The Seaside Lodge

The Seaside Lodge

Kenneth F. Ryan, Sr.

To order additional copies of this book, contact:
Xlibris Corporation
1-888-795-4274
www.Xlibris.com
Orders@Xlibris.com
73105

To my wife Gloria, who helped make this book possible.

1

On the coast of Ireland, approximately eight miles from Dublin, lies a small fishing village. The Irish Sea and her pounding breakers have made this place a wretched spot difficult to get to. There is only one road leading into and out of Downey Lock. The village is made up of mostly anglers and their families. It is a small village with a population of two hundred and twenty-one. The majority of the properties in the village are owned by landlords who reside in England. The people residing in Downey Lock rent from these landlords every three years. There is no written contract between the village people and the wealthy aristocrats, but as long as the people make their payments for the cottages they live in and cause no trouble for the landlords, the villagers usually have no problems. The next village over from Downey Lock is Neary, approximately three miles away.

Most of the anglers have their own boats and go out alone on the Irish Sea. This way, the day's catch will end up just for the one individual boat owner and no sharing will be necessary. Larger boats will at times carry several crewmen, and they assist in the fishing. The more fish you catch, the more money you make. Downey Lock is home to these people and most are adjusted to everyday life. The winters, though usually mild, can occasionally be brutal with the cold wind coming off the Irish Sea. What snow the village does receive seemed to last forever.

There was a school for the children ranging up to age sixteen. After that, students had to leave the village and attend a school outside of Downey Lock. Neary is where most of the children continued their education. The general store, which was located in the center of town, was well stocked with food and other necessities. The Lion Heart Pub was owned by Dean Massey, and like most pubs in Ireland, there was only standing room for customers by early evening. The establishment wasn't that big and had only one room. There was a door in the rear of the building that led to an outhouse so customers could relieve themselves. The walls in this tavern have heard many tales in the past. There is no telling how many pints were served or barrels opened to satisfy the thirsty individuals. The Great War had ended two years before and could serve as a strong topic on any evening for the people who met at the establishment.

Jack Browne, his wife Irene, and their daughter Erin had a four-room cottage with an upstairs loft at the end of town. They were all born in this village and left it only to travel to Dublin for business or on holidays. Jack was a tall, thin man in his midthirties. His thick black hair was long and always combed back, covering his ears. He was a fit man, without an inch of fat on his body. His entire life was his family and keeping them from any discomfort. He kept food on the table by fishing every day with his brother Peter.

Peter, who was several years younger than his brother, lived with his own family, which consisted of his wife Mae and their two children. Jack had turned thirty-four last month. The brothers had their problems getting along with each other. Although the atmosphere had improved, they argued constantly over simple matters. Like his brother, Peter was a tall, strong man who could handle himself with his fists. There were few men in the village that had the interest to tangle with Peter after he had downed his pints at the Lion Heart.

At that time, many people were leaving Ireland and traveling to America. People would write back and tell of the better living conditions there, and if you worked hard, anyone could make a go of it in America. For the past several years, Jack and Irene had saved as much money as possible, preparing for the long journey that would bring them and their daughter to a new homeland and prosperity. Jack and Irene talked over their plans at the Lion Heart while sipping their pints and believing that all would work out well in the end. The winter was ending soon and the weather would be warmer. They wanted to leave near the end of spring or early summer. Little Erin, who was only ten years old, was counting the days they would be at the dock and she would be on the great ship that would take them away. Her father told her so many times what it would be like for her on this great ship riding the big waves. She longed for the adventure that awaited her, for their new home in America, and the new friends she would make.

She was a frail girl with a thin frame and skinny legs. She had her father's raven black hair. Her high cheekbones and cream-colored skin matched her adorable face. Nearly everyone in the village thought she was a beautiful girl. Erin loved the many stories her father told her. He could make up some of the best, including his specialties of the little people that lived in the forest. She loved both her parents, but her father never ceased to amaze her. It seemed that he was the one who was around whenever she needed help. The times she would fall and skin herself, he would kiss the abrasion and make everything in her world perfect again. When he stayed too long at the pub and got drunk, she would go to the Lion Heart and help him home. The songs he would sing while they were walking from the pub always delighted her. He would tell her how beautiful she was and how much he loved her.

She loved to hear his stories about their future in America. Jack would explain to her that there were many job opportunities in America and people could become rich, but he would always assert that he was a fisherman, and he would remain one for as long as he lived. Out on the ocean was the way he would take care of his family. Regardless of the harsh conditions he met at times, he never thought about anything but his love for the sea. His father was a fisherman as was his grandfather. A commitment to the sea was in the Browne's blood. Peter felt the same way since he also was brought up with the sea around him. The brothers wanted nothing else.

Irene met Jack when they were just kids and attended school together. All the families in the village knew each other, and it was difficult to hide any kind of news or business. Since she was a young girl, Irene thought the world of Jack Browne. His boyish good looks and good-hearted manner made a large impression on her. He taught her how to fish and brought her on his boat so she could experience what all fishermen felt when at sea. She too came to love the vast ocean. Although she knew he had a mouth that could spin out lies faster than most drunken sailors, she just loved being with Jack and listening to his silly tales. That was just the way Jack was, and she loved being his companion during these times. She knew that someday she would be by his side forever. By the time she was sixteen, she knew he would be the man who would be her husband. Four years later, when Father Burgess married them in St. Michaels, everyone in the village came to see the grand occasion. Irene was a small girl of twenty with a head of red hair and blue eyes that sparkled like the stars. Her fair skin, petite body, and small hips set her apart from the rest and made her a very attractive young lady. Irene was not only an elegant lassie but was admired by the male population of the village. However, most knew she belonged only to Jack Browne. For twelve years now, they had been together as true mates. Two years after living blissfully together, they had Erin. The only child they would have.

Peter was a hard worker and a good family man. He took to drinking at an early age, believing it made him stronger. Smoking was another habit he enjoyed, particularly at the village pub. A fine glass of ale with a fag tasted ever so good while chatting over the day's events and what news was occurring in the town.

"So when is the departing day for you?" Peter asked his brother. They were both sitting at a table in the center of the pub.

"I believe near the end of spring. Peter, there is nothing here for you either. You know that. This is a poverty-stricken country.

The fishing is not as good as it once was. Soon you will have to change and look for some other kind of work."

Peter thought for a few seconds and told his brother, "This is my home and America scares me. Anyway, Mae would never leave here. We don't have the money and there are other fears too. What happens when you get there? Are you sure of work? What about the living conditions? Suppose you don't get a flat right away, where are you going to sleep?"

Jack didn't have all the answers for Peter's questions, but attempted to reassure him by insisting that if other people had made it over there, why couldn't they.

Erin attended St. Michael's School and was in the fifth grade. When she wasn't home, she was pleased to be at her school. She loved being among her classmates. Sister Mary Ellen, who taught her class, was a pleasant person and quite fond of Erin. The nun was in her early forties and had a petite frame. She had been at the convent of St. Michael's for the last seventeen years. She valued Erin's presence and appreciated being able to teach her. She was a bright child and she learned quickly. The nun knew that Erin came from a poor family, but most of the children were in the same category. They were offspring of fishermen's families. Erin had several girls with whom she was friendly, and they told each other their closest secrets. Erin explained to them that she and her family would soon be on their way to America.

"We are only waiting for the right time to leave, hopefully in the spring," said Erin.

Anna Macery, her best friend, wished her parents would take her away from this isolated place.

"Oh, Erin, I wish I was you right now. You truly have the luck of the Irish," said Anna.

Erin told all her friends they could visit her someday. She promised to keep in touch with them through the mail.

A few days later, during afternoon recess, some boys were kicking around a soccer ball. A tall, skinny boy with long black hair kicked one of his shots hard and struck Erin in the center of her face. Her nose bled and she started to cry. Several children came over and attempted to comfort her. Two nuns supervising the recess also hurried over to attend to her. One of the nuns applied her handkerchief to Erin's nose and told her to lay her head back. The boy who kicked the ball stood in the background and said nothing, but the expression on his face explained how he felt about the incident. He looked as if he was about to cry himself. His lower lip quivered as he tried to speak. One of the sisters looked over at him and gave him a look that would immediately stop a freight train.

The boy spoke softly, saying, "I am deeply sorry. I didn't mean to kick the ball at her."

The youth's face told it all. He meant what he said and everyone could see that it was an accident.

The boy was twelve-year-old Terrance Snow, who lived with his parents in the village. He was in the seventh grade at St. Michael's School and came from one of the poorer families in the village. His father seldom worked, had no real skills, and was taken to drink. Mr. Snow was one of the first to arrive at the pub when the doors opened in the morning. They were not only a poor family, but because of Mr. Snow's refusal to find employment, they were more or less an outcast in the community. What money the Snow family could find usually came from the relief fund that was maintained in the village by the anglers' committee. Arthur Snow was not a very nice man when he was sober, but he could be a troll when drunk. He was repulsive to the people of Downey Locke.

When school ended for the day, Erin was surprised to see Terrance waiting for her outside in the school yard.

"I'm sorry again for kicking the ball into your face and making it bleed," he said. The boy had a half smile on his face as he spoke.

"I feel fine now, and I know that you didn't do it on purpose." She was also smiling now.

They walked out of the school yard, still talking, and headed toward Erin's home. He spoke of her going to America and how he wished he was going too.

"I heard it is wonderful over there and people become rich if they work hard," said Terrance.

"My parents told me the same thing," Erin replied.

As they continued to walk, the boy walked a little faster than Erin, and from behind, she could see two holes in the heel of Terrance's stockings. The boy was wearing knickers with black stockings tucked in just below his knees. The holes were very noticeable and she remembered seeing them in the past when the two were in the school yard. She felt sorry for Terrance not just because he was poor but also appeared unhappy. He was unpopular because of his father. She believed the boy was truthful when he spoke to her.

It was approximately a fifteen-minute walk to Erin's home from her school. He noticed a girl's bicycle leaning against the side of the house with both tires flat.

"Is that your bicycle?" he asked Erin.

"Yes," she said, "but it's broken. The chain keeps falling off."

Erin's mother was standing at the front door and told Erin to come into the house. She didn't acknowledge the boy at all, but simply put her arm around the girl and led her into the house. Once inside, Erin looked out her kitchen window and watched Terrance walk away into the meadow on his way home. She realized just how poor he must be and it deeply saddened her.

It was several days later when Erin saw Terrance in the school yard, and he asked her if he could walk her home again. Although her mother never expressed her feelings about the matter, Erin still knew she didn't like the idea of her associating with the boy. As they walked through the green fields toward her home, the two children talked about school and their after-school activities. Terrance wondered aloud what he would be doing twenty years from now.

"And how about you, Erin?" he asked.

"I suppose I will be somewhere in America. I hope it is New York City. In any case, I will be with my mother and father," she said.

"You know I dislike fishing," he told Erin. "It's okay sometimes to do it for fun, but to do it every day for a living, oh no."

When they reached Erin's home, he took her hand and they walked to an old dilapidated barn that lay on the Browne property. Because of the condition of the barn, it would appear it was built well before the house. When they entered, she saw her bicycle up against the center pole. The tires were no longer flat. The chain was on the bike and it looked brand-new. Terrance told her he repaired the two tires, which had picked up a couple of nails. One had some fragments of glass in it. The girl was stunned when she discovered the bicycle in the barn. She smiled and her eyes sparkled with pure happiness.

"Oh, thank you, Terrance, for repairing my bike! How can I ever thank you for your kindness?"

The boy knew by the expression on her face that he made Erin happy and that alone was enough satisfaction for him. Erin's mother later told her that Terrance had been working on the bike for a day and half and had wanted to surprise her. Although Erin was only ten, her feelings were starting to grow for her older friend. She told her mother that he was a good person and a good friend too, the kind of boy who would help others out of difficult situations if he could.

It was around three in the afternoon when Jack and his brother met at the pub and worked on the day's tally. Their catch of the day had to be brought to the market as soon as possible. But before that, it had to be preserved and packed on ice to stay fresh. One of the local fishermen, Bart McGuire, was standing at the bar. He looked over at the brothers and made some sort of comment that was inaudible. Jack and Peter continued on with their work, paying no attention to anyone else in the establishment. In the past, McGuire had problems with the Browne brothers over specific fishing locations. They never did like each other.

McGuire walked over to their table and spoke in a harsh tone. "So what's going on with the Browne brothers today? Counting all your money I see."

McGuire and his brother Biff had a boat and did some fishing as well. Both wanted the best spots when they went out to sea. The Browne brothers paid no notice to McGuire and continued doing their work. McGuire was starting to burn now and was becoming very disturbed. He didn't appreciate not being recognized by the Browne brothers. Bart McGuire's brother Biff walked into the pub and stood by his brother's side. Bart was bigger than his brother, more rotund and pugnacious. But Biff was no small stiff either.

Bart suddenly stooped over and, with his right hand, grabbed Jack by the hair, pulling him off his chair. Jack landed on the floor several feet away from the McGuire brothers. In a heartbeat, Peter was away from the table, confronting the bullies. Biff swung at Peter but the punch was blocked by the younger Browne, who then landed a right fist into Biff's jaw. Biff fell back when the punch landed, and Peter launched another right hand toward his midsection. It brought Biff down and he rested on one knee attempting to catch his breath. Peter then brought up his right foot and kicked him directly in the face. Biff landed several feet back and was out cold. By this time, Jack was off the floor and came at the other brother. Bart swung at him, but Jack was able to duck under the punch and lay a right cross, a blow that crushed the big man's jaw. It was a devastating punch. It knocked Bart against the entrance door. The hinges popped off and the door landed in the dirt road outside of the pub. Bart now lay unconscious on top of the door. People from the village now came over to the pub to see what had transpired.

Fighting was forbidden inside the pub. Individuals fighting could be banned from the drinking establishment. No one wanted that to happen as the Lion Heart was the only pub in the village. The owner Dean Massey was not working the pub this day and it was a good thing he wasn't. The Browne boys would make good for the damages that occurred. The McGuire brothers were just troublemakers who derived pleasure from hurting others. Some thought it was funny and others thought the McGuire brothers got what they deserved.

The Dublin papers wrote of several bad cases of flu in the city. It was the same flu that was strangling other parts of Europe. London alone had reported several deaths in the last ten days. Officially called the Spanish Flu, it was rapidly spreading everywhere.

While eating supper that night, right after the fight, Jack and Irene decided they would sail for America on June 1.

"It is time," Jack said. "We will leave for Portsmouth and reach America hopefully the same month." Jack acknowledged that there would be some problems, but reminded his family, "With the help of God, we will face them and solve whatever gets in our way."

2

Terrance and Erin were sitting on the grass next to an old ruined mill. They had planned a picnic during the school week and were both excited about it. They discussed their school activities and what was happening in and around the village. Erin was dressed in her special red dress, complimented by a red ribbon in her hair. Terrance was wearing his regular brown knickers and stretched black stockings. As they unwrapped their sandwiches and started eating them, Terrance told Erin how he was going to miss these fine outings. He said he wished they had spent more time together. But the good weather was coming soon and they still had time to explore the outskirts of the village. He intended to bring Erin to the shore and watch the surf striking the rocks by the shoreline. It was a fair day. The sun was beginning to climb higher in the sky each day now. The days were longer and that made living conditions more bearable. Erin was much more mature than Terrance, and she sensed it too.

"We must have another picnic soon," Terrance remarked.

He was fairly sure that Erin was enjoying herself. He told her that everyone in the village was talking about the fight in the Lion Heart and how just about everyone was glad her father and uncle won. As he spoke, he couldn't help but notice how the wind would blow parts of her raven hair across her eyes. Thinking about how adorable she was, he couldn't help but smile. They stayed another hour or so and left for home.

The rain was coming down hard as Irene looked out the kitchen window and some movement in the field caught her eye. It was a figure of someone, but she was not sure if it was a man or a woman. As the figure came closer, she recognized it was the priest from the parish church. Father McVey was a short and rotund man, eyes as green as can be, and a flushed red face some say because of drink. Father McVey could hold his share of ale from the Lion Heart. He also enjoyed his Irish whiskey. Irene greeted him at the door and invited him into her home. He had replaced Father Burgess a little over a year ago.

"Father, what are you doing out in all this rain. Are you trying to catch pneumonia in this cold weather? Come, dry off, and I will make a nice cup of tea for you."

The priest sat at the kitchen table, trying to catch his breath. Walking to the Browne's house from the parish usually only took ten minutes, but because of the heavy rain and wind, it was a tense walk. The priest was a constant visitor to the families in the village. He took interest in what was happening and he cared about the people.

"Irene, I suppose you are wondering why I came over in all this rain but I had to speak to you about Easter."

"Would you fancy a hot biscuit that I just baked this morning, Father?"

She placed the hot biscuits on the center of the table. Looking at them, his mouth watered. Golden brown with a hint of blueberry flavoring, the smell alone made him smile with joy. What a pleasure it was to visit Ms. Browne; she always made such excellent tea, never bitter. The priest asked her if she had plans to work in the church again this Easter, which was only eight days away. Irene confirmed that she would be able to help out for Easter as she had done in the past. She looked forward to it and enjoyed the company of the mothers in the parish. Father McVey thanked her for the tea and delicious biscuits and went on to tell her that Dean Massey was deeply upset about the fight in his pub and wanted those involved to pay for the damages. Irene related to the clergyman that Peter and her husband were going over later today to speak to the pub owner about his damages and make restitution.

"Those two are a pair all right, always looking for a beef. Fighting is in their blood," related Father McVey.

After an hour, the rain let up some and he thanked her once more for the nice snack and tea. He wasn't out the door a minute when the rain started pouring down again. Even the heavens don't care who they drench.

The village fishermen planned to have a social gathering that Friday night. This is one of those occasions that they held several times a year. The entire village would come together for a good time. The men would roast a couple of pigs, fry the day's catch, and roast potatoes and other vegetables. The wives would be in their kitchen roasting choice beefs. Barrels of ale would be brought from the Lion Heart, cooled and ready to drink. Children would play in the field, kicking around a football and annoying the elders. The main topic being spoken during the time was the sickness that was spreading around the United Kingdom and other parts of the world. It was heard that people were dying rapidly in London. Spain also had problems with this type of flu, which some believed originated in America. There was also talk about the many people leaving for America. Some thought it was foolish to leave the place they were born and had lived in for so long with their families. They heard stories that America wasn't all it was cracked up to be, specifically that there was hunger and housing shortage in New York City. Work could be difficult to find there, they were told.

Some of the mothers were sitting at a table eating Mrs. Bradlee's Irish bread. They were discussing the Browne family's upcoming departure for America. The consensus was that it would be difficult to make new friends. Irene was standing close by with her daughter and they were discussing the coming trip. Erin enjoyed these happy times when everyone got together to eat and laugh. She looked for Terrance, but he wasn't around. He probably didn't come and she didn't see his parents either.

Irene looked over and saw her husband and Peter chatting away with Dean Massey. They were laughing over something funny and she wondered what it was. The damages were taken care of and the door was repaired. Not six feet away were the McGuire brothers with their wives, happy as could be. Bart turned and faced the Browne brothers, smiled, and asked that they forget what happened and have a good time. He was sporting a bruise on his right cheek. Jack and Peter said nothing and continued on talking. Just about all the men had pints of Guinness in their hands. Some of these drinking outings may start out with people mending fences and forgetting past troubles, but after several pints, they forget the reconciliation and resume fighting again. As it neared midnight, people left for their homes. The fire that had burnt throughout the evening was left to extinguish itself.

Ireland was a difficult country to live in during these times. There was hardly any work, and if you did not have some sort of trade, you could be hungry most days. At breakfast, Irene complained to her husband Jack that she had difficulty sleeping the night prior. For the past two days, she had a pain in her lower back. She wondered how she got it. Jack didn't think much about it when Irene told him. Later on during the day, she came down with a fever. This still didn't alarm Jack who thought she was coming down with a cold or some kind of virus. Two days later, the fever was at 104 degrees, and now, Jack and Irene were both alarmed that it could be something worse. Jack learned there were a couple of other cases of high fever and back pain striking a young girl and a man of Jack's age in the village. Father McVey, who studied medicine at one of Dublin's largest hospital prior to becoming a Catholic priest, was the only means of medical care in the village. On several occasions, the church basement had to be used as a hospital for the sick. Care workers were called in from a hospital in Neary to assist in an emergency. This was the case when, three years ago, a ship in the harbor struck some rocks and sank. Nine crew members and two passengers had to be brought to the church basement.

Father McVey had no answers for the ill people and suggested that someone contact one of the hospitals in Dublin or Neary.

"We need professional people here immediately and we must not delay," he said. Later, Jack saw Peter coming across the field toward his home.

"How are things, Jack, what can I do to help?"

Jack told him, "She's the same. She is still a very sick woman and I have to find a doctor for her as soon as possible."

"I am here to help you, Jack. Anything I can do, you know that."

"I want to get her over to Neary fast," said Jack.

Jack and Peter sat at the kitchen table. Jack looked over to the bedroom and told Peter she was sleeping now.

"That's all she does really, sleep all day and night."

Erin was upstairs in the loft doing some mending. Jack explained how poor Erin was exhausted from all the work she had to do since her mother's illness.

"She cries daily, worrying about her mother."

It was raining now, and the wind was howling throughout the village, which was nothing new in Downey Locke. The brothers sipped their tea and continued talking. Jack had many thoughts racing through his head. She just had to get well and be herself again. At that point, Francis Mooney came to the door and yelled out Jack's name. Mooney was one of the owners of the general store. He was middle-aged, in his fifties, with thick red hair and bushy eyebrows. Mooney came in from the rain and told Jack and Peter that there was a doctor visiting a nearby house where a little girl was also ill. He was from a hospital in Neary. Jack got up from the table, asked who the girl was and where she lived. Mooney told him what he knew from one of his customers, only that she lived in the red house at the end of Dorset Lane. They were the Shea Family.

Jack immediately went over to the Shea residence and told the doctor about his wife's illness. It was well after dark before Doctor Thornton came to visit Irene. The doctor told Jack that Irene was seriously ill and needed constant attention. He spoke of how people suffering the same symptoms were being admitted to hospitals in Neary and Dublin every day.

"Feed her all the liquids she will take. I will write out a prescription for her. We *must* get that fever down."

The doctor told Jack he would try to return tomorrow. If not, there would be a nurse with instructions there by midmorning. The doctor explained to Jack that most of the hospitals were full to capacity because of this new sickness. He wasn't sure if a bed could be found for Irene at this time. As a result, Irene was bedridden for another two weeks with no change in her condition, except that her face seemed to transform. It became the color of chalk and her breathing was now difficult.

"Come sit near me, Erin," beckoned Irene.

Erin told her mother how much she loved her and assured her that she would recover from this sickness soon. The three of them would be together and would take holiday trips to Dublin. They would have such fun in their new home in New York City. Erin laid her head on her mother's stomach and started to sob, tears soaking the blanket as she continued to cry. She could feel her mother's fingers stroking her hair. Her mother had that wonderful touch of softness. Irene explained to her daughter how she would soon be healthy and ordered her to stop crying as it only made her sadder.

Jack came into the room and was saddened to see his little girl crying and mumbling to her mother. He went into the kitchen and started making some tea for the three of them even though he wasn't sure if Irene would be able to drink hers. Erin was becoming sleepy as she lay on her mother, feeling her stroke her hair. Suddenly, the stroking of her hair stopped and she felt only the weight of her mother's hand on her head. Jack heard his daughter scream out for him. Irene was lying on her back with her eyes open. She had drawn her last breath.

Like most wakes in Downey Locke, Irene was laid out in the parlor of her home. Erin sat next to her mother and never left her side while the many villagers passed by her. Jack believed his world had come to an end. Father McVey attempted to comfort Jack and his daughter and blessed those in attendance. It was a typical Irish wake. Several mourners gathered in the kitchen with their share of whiskey. Some went outside and sat on the ground next to the barn. Most of the mothers kept their distance from the men who were drinking. It's an ancient tradition for people to drink at an Irish wake. Father McVey himself made it to the kitchen and indulged in a couple of pints. The two McGuire brothers appeared and offered their respects.

The younger brother told Jack, "I'm sorry for your trouble." This is an old Irish proverb used at most Irish wakes and funerals. The kitchen table was laid out with delicious-looking food brought by the neighbors: fish cakes, potato salads, and assorted cuts of meats. Fresh Irish soda breads permeated the room with their grand aroma. Jack left the parlor and came into the kitchen. Leaning against the ice chest, he considered the kindness and sympathy of all who had come to offer condolences. Peter came over and handed him a glass of whiskey.

He told him, "Drink this. It will make you feel better inside."

Jack walked over to the door leading into the parlor and noticed the Snow boy talking to Erin. He patted her head and she smiled for the first time the entire evening. The parlor was full of people. No one had left since they first arrived.

The funeral was scheduled for ten the following morning. It started raining early in the morning, and by the time everyone was inside the church, it was raining even harder. Following the mass, the coffin was carried down the stone steps and placed into the horse-drawn wagon. While the wagon was slowly moving down the street leading to St. Mary's Cemetery, you could hear the horse's hoofbeats echoing along the cobblestone street. People walked closely behind, and some were showing their grief by sobbing and holding their handkerchief.

Upon arriving at the cemetery, Father McVey said a few prayers and closed with the simple request, "May she rest in peace."

There was no returning to Jack's house for refreshments as he wanted to be alone with his daughter.

He became a constant visitor to Irene's grave. On a typical day, he would usually arrive right after breakfast. Talking to her in the same way he did when she was sitting across from him at the kitchen table, he would ask her why she left them in such a hurry. Should he and Erin make the trip to America? He still trusted her advice. Every visit made it easier to return for the next. He sensed she responded to everything they discussed. Most times, but not always, he let himself cry. While crying made him feel better, the sadness was a torment.

He had many things to talk over with Erin, especially their trip to America. Would it be fundamentally sound to make the trip now, given Irene's recent passing? The death and funeral had left them with a shortage of money after Jack bought her a grand burial stone and a casket made of mahogany. Jack recalled Irene's deathbed statement telling him to go to America with their daughter. They needed more money however, so Jack decided to work out on the sea with Peter for a few more months. Perhaps July or August would be a better time. It would be warmer in New York and would provide him a better chance of finding work. Jack heard so many different stories relating to finding employment that he didn't know who to believe. It was one of his biggest concerns.

Erin was happy about the delay as she told her father, "Whatever you decide is fine with me." She confided to him that she would miss Downey Locke and her friends.

3

The month of April continued to be cold and wet. Jack and Peter froze while hauling in their catch during their trips, but they made enough money so Jack could make plans to leave by the middle of summer. With the coming of summer and school letting out, most people were jolly in Downey Locke. They were talking about going to Dublin for some excitement and good times. Jack's mind was on another destination, and this excited him. He now had $210 in America money. Tomorrow, he would start gathering the proper papers he needed such as passports and other means of identification so there would be no problems while on the streets of America. Jack knew the voyage alone would cost $100 for both of them. They had to pass inspection at Ellis Island, the Port of New York, and this required that they be in excellent health, which they were.

After school, Terrance was waiting for Erin out on the front lawn. He told Erin that his father was acting up more than ever now, and it was disturbing his mother. The drinking was still a daily occurrence, but now it was starting earlier in the morning.

"How I wish I was going to America too. I would love to get away from this terrible environment here in Downey Lock. No one speaks to me and I am always alone. You're the only true friend I have."

Erin reminded her friend that she would be leaving for America soon.

"I will miss you, Terrance. You're a good lad. Who knows, maybe you will be able to come someday, and we will meet again and talk about the old days here in Downey Lock."

In mid-August, Jack and his daughter stood on the pier admiring the big ship that would take them across the Atlantic Ocean and into their new dreams. Their passage was down at the bottom of the ship. It was third class. The accommodations weren't the best, but they would make the necessary adjustments. It didn't matter as long as they were on their way to the land of opportunity. It was after the evening meal when the passengers would join together and have fun. A couple of them played musical instruments and there was singing and dancing throughout the night. After twelve days at sea, rumors flew around the ship that they should see land sometime that afternoon. Consequently, there were not many passengers inside of their cabins at 1:00 p.m. It was a beautiful day and the sun was high in the sky. It was hot and there was no breeze at all, but no one was complaining. A little after 3:00 p.m., someone yelled out that they saw the statue. Erin shouted to her father she wanted to see it—*the lady statue holding a lamp.*

Orientation was held at a large brick building near the southern part of Ellis Island. They learned the health inspection would begin immediately upon entrance to the hospital. No one would be allowed to stay in America if they didn't pass both the mental and physical examinations. If you had twenty American dollars per person, you didn't need a sponsor. Both Jack and Erin had that amount and more. The following morning, they were briefed about their new homeland and what they could expect as they walked the streets of America. The room was very large and it held hundreds of immigrants seeking a new life. Jack recognized some of the people in the hall after seeing them on the ship. A woman stood on a platform and spoke into a microphone. She instructed them that the first thing they were to do was seek employment.

She also said, "Your sponsor, if you have one, can assist you in this matter. You should have already made arrangements regarding your living accommodations. Those of you that have not, I recommend you read the bulletin board at the entrance of the building. It will explain everything you need to know about seeking a place to live."

The lady went on to tell them of an Irish house down on the east side that took in emergency cases only. No exceptions. It was called Fourth Clover and the address was listed on the bulletin board. You were limited to how long you could stay at this residence. After ten days, you were asked to leave. It cost a dollar a day.

When Jack and Erin stepped onto the ferry that would take them to the most southern tip of Manhattan, there was nothing but joy expressed by both. Jack kept his money in the right front pocket of his trousers. Any change he kept in his left side pocket. This was a habit to which he had become accustomed. When they reached Battery Park, they had made it to their final destination.

Jack had a small suitcase by his side and Erin was carrying a small bag with her belongings. They stopped by a bench and sat down to rest. Jack held his daughter's hand and smiled at her, telling her how lucky they were that they managed to make it here to America.

"Darling, how I miss your mother right now. But she is looking down at us, Erin, and she is happy for us."

Erin tried to hide her tears but failed. She hugged her father and told him she loved him very much. Jack took her hand and looked for the bulletin boards he was told were in Battery Park. These contained the information they needed to find the Fourth Clover. As they walked by the Brooklyn Bridge, Erin marveled at the magnificent structure. Finally, they reached a building whose entryway contained a large green clover; they had found the house that would keep them safe for the night. Peering out the window of their one-room flat, one could see the Brooklyn Bridge with the many automobiles and horse-drawn carriages moving steadily along it. It amazed Erin how crowded it was in New York City. Everyone walked so fast and people were riding bicycles everywhere. People walking on the Brooklyn Bridge were dodging the many bikes and scooters that came upon them.

Jack asked some of the residents at the Fourth Clover whether there were any jobs in the area. They too were looking for employment and knew only that work was scarce in the big city. Jack made inquiries regarding commercial fishing and received similar results. Most of the fish were brought in by trucks from New England and Maryland. The docks surrounding the East River where the large ships made port carried mostly hard goods.

Radios and kitchen appliances loaded into large cartons were removed from the ships every day. The docks were controlled by the unions and the dockworkers. Posted on poles were signs reading, No Help Wanted and All Irish Need Not Apply. Jack and Erin walked the streets of the city, making acquaintances with people and sizing up the neighborhood. Jack had a strange feeling that work might be a problem on the East Side. He worried whether the entire city was like the East Side. He was warned on a couple of occasions that if he found a job to hold on to it. Don't lose it.

After several days wandering the East Side searching for employment, he and Erin were becoming discouraged. There were shipping docks on the West Side of the city bordering the Hudson River, but these docks were also run by the union. It seemed as though the union had a clamp on all longshoremen and ruled who could work the docks.

Since prohibition was in effect, it was difficult to get a drink of any kind. Jack often thought what an idiotic law it was. This would never happen in Ireland. He was told of a place adjacent to the bridge where you could purchase alcoholic beverages, but only if you were a member. The cover charge was a dollar and the liquor was pricey. He knew his funds were getting low, so he intended to have only one beer, two at most. Anyway, the change would do him good and he hadn't had a drink since leaving Ireland. It was late August and very hot in lower Manhattan, as it usually is this time of year. It was only 7:00 p.m. and the sun was still high in the sky. Jack was a bright fellow; he just lacked good old common sense at times.

Jack waited until a middle-aged gent came to the club door. Then he saw the man knock and wait for a moment. The man was led in and the door closed. Jack approached the club door, knocked, and waited. Looking through a small square hole, he gave the man a dollar. Jack was allowed inside the establishment and he walked to the bar. The place was just as packed as the Lion Heart on a Saturday night. Jack reassuringly patted his right front pocket where he kept his money, a habit of which he could not rid himself. He was doing this since he was a young boy. Sitting at a table with a bottle of whiskey on it, near the rear door of the club, were two men. One was fat and it appeared as though he hadn't shaved in over a week. The right side of his face was blemished with red marks and pimples. He had a head full of unruly red hair and hands that a professional wrestler would be proud of.

The fat man glanced over to the man sitting next to him and said with a smile, "Greenhorn." He repeated "right off the boat" and laughed out loud.

His friend roared with laughter and said, "You saw where the bucks are?"

"Oh yeah, he wanted us to know and even showed us."

The fat individual was Charlie Hawkins, born and bred right here in Manhattan. People called him the Shark, a nickname that he loved and fit him well. His friend was called Perrent. No one knew his last name, and most weren't sure if it was his first or last name. Not that anyone cared. These scumbags were two horrible people. They had the reputation of not only conning you and cheating you out of your last penny, but of inflicting bodily harm. From the time Jack walked into the club and ordered his drink, he was observed by both of these characters as easy pickings. Perrent left the table, approached the bar, and stood next to Jack. The bar was full of people talking at the same time. Jack thought his whiskey was sour tasting. Perrent looked at the bartender and ordered a drink. Perrent knew that he and the bartender were on the same page. The log was thrown in the fire and now they just waited for it to burn.

Erin had made just a few friends while at the Clover House and one of them was a man named Percy Williams, the house handyman. He was a short man with sleepy eyes, a round face, and a rather large belly. During the several days since he knew Erin, he had become fond of her. He explained that his work here in the house meant he had to repair whatever got broken. He also took care of the outside of the house. As he spoke, he would glance over to her every now and then. He thought the girl seemed lonely and scared. "You have to make friends, Erin. Take a walk on the bridge over to Brooklyn. Soon you will be in school and that's where you will make new friends. At age ten and alone with just your father in a new world, things have to be taken with care."

She was not sure if she should take the handyman's advice and walk over to Brooklyn. She was not even sure if she liked the man. She remembered her father's many warnings to not trust anyone. He was to decide with whom she could become friendly. Williams had a small room down in the cellar of the establishment. No one was allowed down in the cellar, and that was all right with Erin as it was dark and spooky down there. Erin wondered where her father was. She knew there were no barrooms available in New York.

Perrent turned to look at Jack and asked him if he was from the city. Jack spoke softly and told him that he was.

Perrent said, "Please allow me to buy you a beer."

Jack noticed a big smile on the stranger's face. The bartender drew two draft beers and placed them in front of the men, without any expression on his stoic face.

"So how long have you been here in the city?" Perrent asked.

A suspicious person by nature, Jack was now curious as to why this individual was being so friendly toward him. Jack saw prying eyes and he reminded himself to be careful with this mate. Jack continued to make small talk with Perrent, leaving out any personal information or mention of his future plans. The bartender had placed two more beers and two shot glasses of whiskey on the bar before them. Jack knew he didn't order the drinks and wondered why the bartender had given away free alcohol.

He didn't ignore the whiskey, but rather gulped it down and then sipped his beer chaser until the glass was empty. The bartender was at the other end of the bar talking to another customer. It was the Shark he was speaking with and both of them looked over at Jack and Perrent. Jack saw them for a second or two but thought nothing of it. Perrent asked him again how long he had been in New York. Jack told him not that long. Perrent said he had never seen him in this place before and went on about how difficult it was to get hold of a drink since prohibition had arrived.

"Are you working yet?" pried Perrent. "It's difficult to find work here, especially if you don't know anyone of influence."

Perrent noticed that Hawkins had returned to their table.

"You are a man of few words, my friend."

This statement by Perrent took Jack by surprise. Perrent then said if Jack was looking for work, he might be able to help him.

"But I think you are one of those independent guys who like to make it on their own. This is New York and it can eat you up very fast if you don't know what is going on. It's nice to have a friend you can trust here, someone who can show you around and help you make decisions. Know what I mean?"

Jack just listened to the man and said nothing. There were more beers and shots on the bar. He drank them down without stopping.

Perrent asked Jack to join him at his table. After hesitating for a moment, Jack decided to see what else Perrent had to offer. Jack could hold his liquor with the best drinkers in Downey Lock. He saw no problems with this stranger as long as he stayed sober. The other man sitting at the table was introduced by Perrent as Charlie Hawkins.

"What is your name again?" asked Perrent.

"Jack Browne," replied Jack.

Jack remembered it was Hawkins who he saw talking to the bartender earlier.

"It's my pleasure to meet you. Any friend of Perrent is a friend of mine," said Hawkins

Hawkins gave out one of the roaring laughs for which he was known. His eyes were glassy from the booze.

He shouted out to a waiter who stood nearby, "More drinks over here! Hurry, man!"

The drinks arrived and again Jack wasn't asked to pay. He had been in this tavern for several hours and had yet to pay for a single drink. Beers and shots of American whiskey were placed on the table. He noticed the time on the clock was 8:30 p.m. Where had the time gone? He knew that Erin was safe at the Clover House and she would be taken care of by the people there, so he continued to drink and felt quite good considering the amount of alcohol he consumed. They drank for several more hours and Jack still had not paid for a single drink. Charlie told him not to worry about the money, that everything would be put on his tab.

"I have a running bill in this tavern, which I pay at the end of every month." Again, he roared with laughter. By this time, it was after 11:00 p.m. and near closing time. After rising from his chair, Jack began to believe that these people were not as bad as he had originally thought. He had not spent a nickel for a drink all evening. The bar was still full and the piano player continued to play. Jack took a few steps toward the door but then had to stop. He leaned against a table. Something was wrong; he didn't feel right. He was nauseous and he felt dizzy. Someone was assisting him out of the drinking establishment. He couldn't distinguish who he was. He then imagined he saw Hawkins near the door smiling at him. Suddenly, he was alone and so drunk he could barely keep his balance.

He heard someone ask, "Mister, are you okay?"

The voice was not clear and he couldn't determine if it belonged to a man or a woman. He could feel someone leading him as he stumbled along. Everything was a blur. He couldn't reason with himself. There was nothing but darkness.

4

Earlier that afternoon, Erin was on her way back from the Brooklyn side of the bridge after what she deemed an enjoyable walk. The view from the north left her in awe of Manhattan's sheer size. They were constructing buildings that seemed to reach the sky. Along the river, there was smoke coming from a section on the East Side. Trucks entered and left the dirt road from where the smoke arose. Then, she realized it was the city dump. With her sense of awe shattered, she walked to the Clover House and went to her room. She wondered where her father was and decided he was probably still out looking for work. She knew he was disgusted and disappointed that he did not have a job yet. A few minutes later, she went to the kitchen and spoke to the cook, who prepared her a sandwich. As she enjoyed her lunch, the two spoke about his days with the navy. Born in England, he had joined the U. S. Navy upon his arrival from Kent. He became a cook while on board ships, where he was forced to learn quickly from solely on-the-job training. She asked him what kind of sandwich he made for her as it was really tasty.

"Corned beef. It goes really good with cabbage," he answered. Erin explained how people in Ireland eat cabbage almost every day.

"Cabbage stuffed with meat and also just stuffed cabbage and potatoes."

Erin returned to her room and sat on her bed to wait for her dad. He had been gone since early afternoon. She was tired, and as soon as she lay on her bed, she fell asleep. When Erin awoke the following morning, her father was still not home. This upset her because she knew her father would never stay away from her overnight. She dressed quickly and went outside to look for him. It was raining lightly and it appeared the sky was brightening. She asked the few people she knew about her father. She talked to several of the peddlers and fruit venders on the street. Jack Browne had not been seen.

As she walked back to the Clover House, she saw a policeman coming out of the front door. He stopped and asked her if she was Erin Browne and she replied she was. He told her that he just brought her father upstairs.

"He's resting now. He was injured last night."

When Erin entered their room, she saw a man in plainclothes talking to her father. She heard her father tell the detective he was beaten and robbed during the night. He never mentioned he had been drinking at a Speakeasy club earlier. Jack's eyes sparkled when he saw his daughter. He told the detective all the money he had, which was seventy-two dollars, was stolen. He stated that he needed to get the money back right away. It was all the money he had since he couldn't find work. The detective told him the money was gone for good and probably already spent.

"Even if I make an arrest, by this time, the money was spent on illegal liquor." Jack wanted to mention the two culprits he met inside the club. The police probably knew the two, but then he would be placing himself in jeopardy. He would have to find them himself and make them return his money.

Erin could see a black bruise under her father's right eye. She also heard him say he had four stitches in the rear of his head. Jack knew he was intoxicated not only by the booze he drank, but also some drug mixed inside the alcohol. This implicated the bartender who prepared the drinks. Since Jack wouldn't identify anyone, there wasn't much the police could do about the incident. The detective was suspicious of Jack's statement and knew he was withholding information about his robbery.

The detective said, "The cop on the beat finds you at 3:00 a.m. lying unconscious in an alley and you don't know how you got there. You received a head wound and a bruised right eye. You're admitted overnight to the hospital and you might have to return for more treatment. There is a lot here I don't understand."

The detective left and Jack moved over to the window and saw him talking outside to the uniformed policeman who, after a second, started shaking his head. With tears in her eyes, Erin went over to her father and hugged him. They both began to cry. Although her father didn't tell her all the particulars regarding the incident, she had a pretty good idea of what occurred during last night's escapades. She certainly was happy her dad was not seriously injured, but could it be true he lost all his money? She knew that a precarious future lay ahead of them. Erin offered her father the eight dollars remaining in her savings.

He warned her, "Keep it safe. We are going to need it."

Jack made several attempts to get back into the unnamed club but was unsuccessful. Each time he returned, there was a new man at the door and Jack was told he was wasting his time trying to get back in. He waited for hours outside the building searching for the two culprits that stole his money. He told his story to anyone that took the time to listen. Some knew who he was talking about, but didn't want to get involved so they wouldn't offer him any information. They knew better than to discuss a situation such as this. The ones that would speak about the matter suggested that he forget it ever occurred. One friend told him not to make matters worse as he could end up losing his life.

During the day, Jack continued to look for work. During the evening, Jack and Erin would sit outside on the stoop and discuss their future, which at this point looked bleak. With the days passing by, Jack knew they would have to leave Clover House and seek new arrangements. What money they had begun their journey with was now gone with the exception of some small change. Erin asked Jack if things would be better if they crossed over the bridge into Brooklyn. Jack knew it would be the same in Brooklyn as Manhattan. New York was just a hard city to find work. Jack missed Irene; it just wasn't the same without her. He would have had better luck with her by his side. Feeling awful that he let Erin down, he was convinced that she considered him a complete imbecile for losing the only funds they had saved for so long.

The proprietor of the Clover House, Mrs. Carbet Rominsky, was waiting for Jack and Erin when they came in through the front door. She was a plump Russian woman, with graying hair pulled back into a bun. A reputation as a no-nonsense individual who took no guff from anyone, Rominsky called out to Jack as he and Erin walked toward the staircase. "You owe me for last night's lodging and for today too." Her face now was the color of a red rose and her eyes sparked with anger. She never smiled; she hated the world. A hard-boiled woman who never had a trusted friend her entire life, she married twice, with both marriages failing.

Jack started to explain how he would have the money the following morning.

"We have our rules and regulations here and they have never been broken in the past. Let me have your key, please," she said.

Jack placed the key into the hand of the woman. Jack and Erin walked out through the front door onto the street. It started raining again. They walked down by the East River. Nothing was said between them. There was nothing but disgust on Jack's face. They continued walking along a street on the riverbank. There was a cool breeze coming off the river. It was dark now and raining really hard. They needed shelter for the night. Erin was shivering as she wore no outer garments. Jack wished she had some sort of wrap to protect her from the cold rain. They stood under a street lamp and rested for a moment or two. The rapid rain was now drenching the street under them as well as their bodies.

Jack held his daughter's hand and told her, "We will go under the bridge to get out of the rain."

There were stone steps leading down to the ground area. They walked beneath the bridge, and Erin stared in wonder at the large stone pillars that were supporting the bridge. At least there was relief from the rain under the bridge. Jack asked Erin if she was feeling better, and she nodded with a smile. Jack noticed three brick buildings approximately fifty feet away from the river that appeared to have been there for many years. He thought these buildings must have been for the people working on the bridge or perhaps storage for supplies and materials for the construction of the bridge. Jack peered inside one of the windows but couldn't see anything because of the rain and aging glass. The door had no lock. Jack had some difficulty opening the door because of deterioration that had accumulated. He pushed hard a couple of times and the door gave in. He walked inside and saw it was empty except for several beer cans. One of the rear windows contained no glass. It had a terrible odor reminiscent of the smell of an embalming room. It prompted Jack to wonder if someone had indeed died there and the smell had lingered on, so he tried the next building where the door was also unlocked. He entered with no trouble and again saw nothing inside. There were some bricks that had fallen away and lay on the wooden floor. Under one of the windows, he saw where someone had defecated on the floor. It hadn't been there that long.

The last building was locked. He couldn't see inside, so he decided to break the lock on the door. He picked up a large rock from the ground, and after several attempts the lock broke and he entered the edifice. The structure was empty, all the windows were intact, and it appeared fairly clean. Erin was now down by the river watching the boats. He called her and told her they would be staying the night inside this building. The door had a latch on the inside, which Jack secured. Erin sat on the wooden floor with her face in her hands. The rain still pounded away on the roof, and she wished she could be anywhere but this horrible place. Jack looked outside the window and counted seven boats on the East River. He wondered if any of them were fishing boats. He sat down next to his daughter and hugged her close. Within minutes, she was fast asleep in his arms. What a terrible mess, he thought to himself. He lay back with Erin in his arms and waited for sleep. But he knew this was going to be a sleepless night.

5

Otto Rhineheart was a German from a small town on the Swiss border called Voyhaim. He was born into an aristocratic family. His father owned two factories, which assisted in the war effort. They manufactured textile goods that helped clothe the German soldiers. The Rhinehearts had a large estate, which included a mansion with thirty rooms and three motorcars. When young Otto finished his schooling in Voyhaim, his father sent him to Harvard to further his education. When it was completed, he never returned to Germany. Instead, he and a friend started a boat-building business in the city of Boston. At first, the boats were small, but as the business improved, they built larger vessels, working their way toward the construction of ships that left for the high seas.

Rhineheart married and had five children. The family resided in the upper-scale section of Boston. The house was newly constructed with the most up to date amenities. Rhineheart was a slightly built man with brown hair and a fair complexion. He was always immaculate and elegantly dressed. He spoke both English and German fluently. Now, at age fifty-three, he felt he had accomplished just about what he intended to do in life. His business was doing fine and he was in good health. His wife Etta, who he married several years after leaving Harvard, was a good wife and mother. Yet Rhineheart had one more venture that he couldn't keep out of his mind. He had to complete this last conquest before he would be satisfied. For the last three years, his wife Etta had been after him to get them out of the city of Boston during the summer. She wanted her own second home on the ocean. She dreamed of a place where her children could go to the beach and be comfortable during the hot summer months, a place where they could go swimming and bring their friends. Also, Otto could invite his own friends there from Boston and have them relax overnight. The summer months were intolerable in the city of Boston.

Between Revere and Lynn on the North Shore of Boston lies a stretch of land right on the Massachusetts coast called Snugport. In the past, Otto had visited this isolated portion of land and even did some fishing. Etta first thought about Cape Cod being a nice spot for a summer home. Otto told her it was too far from Boston where he worked. One of the added benefits of Snugport was that they could either take the train right into the area or drive down route 1-A, which was just a thirty-minute ride to their destination. Otto purchased a little over an acre of land and it was there that he intended to build his new summer home. There was another feature that lured the German to this small village. Approximately a half mile from shore was an island with a lighthouse on it. The foghorn could be heard for miles. The light from the tower could be seen all the way to the port of Boston. It was a beautiful sight, and the people of the village loved it when the light shone to inform ships on the water of the dangerous rocks close by. The lighthouse was built in 1810 and had an attendant throughout the years. Before the lighthouse was constructed, several ships had struck some of the rocks near the shore and sunk. When Rhineheart was informed of the lighthouse's history, it made him all that more anxious to purchase the land and start building.

The village could be a haven for fog most of the time. The house was completed within two years and it stood proudly on a cliff with a seventy-five-foot drop to the ground. A staircase was built with railings on both sides so people could reach the beach. The dwelling contained five bedrooms and three up to date bathrooms. It was a large house, the largest one north of Boston. A porch wrapped around its perimeter. In addition, once you walked down the several cement steps, you found yourself in a courtyard that surrounded the front of the house. The courtyard had a small pond, which contained several fish and a waterfall. The flower garden was always well kept and maintained. Two large stone pillars guarded the front entrance. Otto and his family had many happy times living in their oceanfront home.

Five years after the house was built, Otto suffered a stroke while lying on the beach. Two days later, he died. The house was later sold to a lawyer from New Jersey who lived there with his wife and three children. They later divorced and the house was left vacant for some time. The town started developing as new businesses were opened, and several more homes were built in the area. The town of Snugport was growing fast.

Voices outside awakened Jack; he then saw that Erin was already up and out of the building. Down by the river, Erin was talking to a terrible-looking man whom Jack had never seen before. Approximately in his late forties, the stranger was dressed in dirty black trousers, shabby socks, and a white shirt that had turned almost completely brown. He sported a three-day beard and his fingers were visibly grimy. It was clear that the man had not been near water for some time. Beside him, a red wagon held a collection of junk. Erin told her father she just met Mr. Tyler and that he made his way collecting odd things.

The man stood fast with a smile on his face and said, "You have a sweet little girl here. You are a fortunate man."

The man looked disgusting to Jack, but he tried to be pleasant toward the wayward individual. He introduced himself to Jack as Conlon Tyler and explained that he had been working the banks of the East River for the past five years or so. Originally from Philadelphia, he now lived here in the city. Tyler, as he was talking to Jack and Erin, would now and then look over to the shelter where the two spent the night. He sensed these two had as many problems as he. As Tyler continued to speak, Jack ascertained Mr. Tyler was no fool. Outside of his bad clothing and hygiene, the man was polite while talking to both Jack and Erin. He spoke well, and Jack was aware that Mr. Tyler knew he and Erin spent the night in the brick building. However, Jack wasn't even sure if Tyler was this man's real name. He didn't trust him.

"I am really just a man scratching out a buck with this wagon of mine," said Tyler.

Tyler told Jack what junk he picked up he later sold—bottles, cans, anything that he could sell and make a dollar. Jack learned from his past to be on guard against everyone. He kept a keen eye on Tyler as he continued talking about making money. After a while, Jack revealed that after a streak of bad luck he was low on funds, in short, that they had no money and no place to stay the night. Tyler asked him if he had gone to the IRA for assistance.

"Are you talking about the Irish Republic Army," asked Jack with a grin on his face.

"No no, I am speaking about the Irish Republic Association. They help down and out Irish, especially newcomers to America. They are funded by successful Irish groups here in New York."

"No one told me anything about this organization. Even when we were first docked in the harbor and throughout all the briefings, nothing was said about it," said Jack.

Tyler had learned of the place over a year ago from other Irishmen.

"A few of my friends are Irish, and they have been there a few times and always made out well. I can take you there. It is over on Second Ave."

Tyler told him he and his daughter could stay the night at his place not far from here.

"If you make a score at the Irish place, we will have a nice dinner. You may be able to claim food vouchers since you are somewhat desperate."

Jack still didn't know if he was speaking the truth. He thanked Tyler for the offer of staying at his home for the night. Jack knew nothing of this individual and still didn't trust him, but there was something about his attitude and the way he expressed himself that kept Jack interested in him. There were now several others walking along the bank of the river. A couple of them nodded to Jack and kept walking. Jack thanked Tyler again for his thoughtfulness, took Erin's hand, and proceeded to walk away from him.

A woman came up to him to say, "I heard what Tyler was saying to you. You know he lives in the city dump about a mile from here next to the river. He has what really is nothing but a cardboard shack. You would do well to take your little girl away from him and not listen to any of his promises."

Suddenly another person appeared, a man perhaps in his early fifties, and spoke to Jack. "Tyler is okay. He has never hurt nor even angered anyone I know."

Jack was able to learn from these people that the IRA was located just where Tyler said it was, Second Avenue at Fourteenth Street. Jack had to get some food soon as he knew Erin must be starving. Neither had eaten since early yesterday.

There was a long wait at the IRA. The line was out the door.

"Expect over an hour wait," said the young lady at the desk.

She wore glasses and never looked up at Jack the entire time he spoke. She wasn't that old, perhaps in her late thirties, but she wore a red dress that was much too tight on her. Jack asked if she thought he would receive some assistance as he was in desperate need of help. She was flipping through some papers and still paid him no attention.

The woman answered, "I have no idea and everyone that comes in through this front door is desperate."

She now showed some anger on her face and said, "Take a seat please and wait your turn."

Erin was standing by his right side. Jack noticed that the nameplate on her desk read *Jill Pleasant*. Jack whispered to Erin "Check out the name on the desk." Erin started giggling. Jack wondered how such a mean bitch could end up with such a last name. After some time, the girl walked over to Jack and handed him some paperwork.

She said, "Don't miss any of the questions and be sure to fill everything out."

An hour and thirty minutes later, Jack's turn finally came. He and Erin entered a small office area where there sat a lady in her sixties with no expression on her face whatsoever. *Another prude*, thought Jack. She had short salt-and-pepper hair and wore a blue-and-black dress that fit her nicely.

"Please take a seat and relax, both of you," she said.

Her name was Grace Fleming and she was the assistant administrator for the IRA. She checked the screening papers Jack completed. He requested no money only food and lodging until he got a job and was earning his own way. Jack told the woman he would do any kind of work to earn a living.

"Why don't you have any cash? What happened to it? Why have you reached such a desperate condition?" asked Ms. Fleming.

Jack didn't want to lie, but he knew this woman wouldn't like to hear how he lost his money in an unauthorized saloon. Jack held his daughter's hand and told the woman he had received some very bad advice.

"Please," Erin implored to Mrs. Fleming sitting across from her, "can you help us just this once?"

The lady asked Jack of his occupation, and he relayed to her that he was a fisherman and had been one since he was a young boy in Ireland.

During the interview, Jack sensed that Mrs. Fleming was sympathetic. She kept an eye on Erin while speaking and couldn't help noticing her perfect features. She could tell that, when the girl reached adulthood, she would be charming as well as beautiful.

"I am going to give you a food voucher. It will be made out to you and your daughter in the amount of five dollars as well as a place to stay for seven days. After seven days, the hotel voucher will be void. You should be working and on your own by then," she said.

Jack was stunned and grateful. Fleming could see it in his eyes.

"I thank you, miss, for your generosity and my daughter thanks you too." Grace Fleming told Jack he was to report back to the IRA every other day. "You are to look for employment every day. Check the papers and look for signs in workshops. You are to go to the Basil Hotel on Third Avenue, three blocks uptown. Mr. Browne, be back here to give a report of your activities the day after tomorrow. There is very little fishing here in Manhattan," she warned Jack.

Forever grateful they both thanked the kind lady. Jack took Erin's hand and they walked out of the building. Both had smiles on their faces, and inside, they felt joyful.

6

Jack and Erin were excited to see their new room. It was one room with cold water only. They shared the bathroom with the other guests on the fifth floor. They immediately went grocery shopping, and among their purchases were American-made cigarettes for Jack. He hadn't had a smoke in three days. A couple of days later, Jack reported to the IRA building as he was ordered. He spoke with another person there as Grace was not at her desk. He thought this woman might have doubted his word on seeking work, but he knew he was out there looking and so did Erin.

A little after three in the afternoon, he was notified by the desk clerk that there was a telephone call for him. Grace Fleming was on the other line and waited while he picked up.

She said, "Mr. Browne, can you clean fish? Have you ever filleted fish after catching them? There is a fishing company looking for an experienced fillet man."

Jack jumped at the opportunity and said he could skin anything. She ordered him to come see her on the second floor where she would give him all the details for the job. After thanking Grace Fleming, he went directly to the hotel room to tell Erin. He was to report for work tomorrow morning at 4:00 a. m. and ask for a Mr. Spencer.

Henry Spencer was a tall man over six feet four and weighed two hundred and thirty pounds. He was built like a truck. His eyebrows were crooked as they went up straight over his eyes. His teeth were bad and he was known for his putrid breath. His blondish hair was thinning on top. His face was gross as he had a couple of warts on his nose. He was a quick-tempered individual. He was the manager of the Manhattan Clam and Fish Co. on First Avenue, where he started at age fourteen and had remained for twenty-five years. A rude individual, he didn't like many people. As an aggressive worker, his attitude left him disliked by his coworkers and gained him a reputation as a nefarious individual, the type who would fire an employee in a heartbeat if that person so much as angered him. For the past eight years now, he was in charge of the fishing plant and responsible for moving the fish to their destinations. He was directly in charge of hiring and firing people.

Jack got to the fishing plant a little early, 3:45 a.m. A full moon was still in the sky, but it was already hot and humid. Jack looked through the pane glass door and saw a burly-type man sitting at a desk. He knocked lightly on the glass and waited for a response from the man who waved at him to come in. Spencer sat back in his swivel chair and looked at the man standing in front of him.

"I'm Jack Browne," Jack said.

Spencer thought to himself, *Another Irish Mick.*

Jack's application said he was an experienced fillet man, but Spencer told him he would know immediately if Jack was experienced with a knife.

"You Irish people have a bad reputation. You are known to drink too much, be lazy, and terribly unreliable."

He brought Jack out to the rear of the plant where the employees accomplished most of the work. The smell hit Jack immediately. It was the smell his nostrils hadn't breathed in some time, the smell of fresh fish that Jack loved. Spencer placed a bucket of ice on a table that was covered with white paper. Beside the bucket were several knives. Spencer told him to go to work. He wanted Jack to skin the fish. There is a certain way to do this particular kind of work and one must be skillful at it. Spencer knew it didn't take the average cutter anymore than a couple of minutes to complete one fish. Jack had been doing this kind of work all his life and zipped right through filleting the fish as Spencer watched with a keen eye. He was surprised how well Jack was doing. There was no doubt Jack had experience in filleting fish. But Jack knew this hard-boiled man had no use for him. There had to be at least seven or eight other workers employed at the fish plant.

After working there several hours, Jack realized Spencer was a hated man. His nickname was the Brute. Workers were terrified of him. They never knew when they would be out of a job. His method was fear and he liked to keep his employees wondering. But Jack held his own and continued to satisfy Spencer. When Jack wasn't cutting fish, he was doing other work. The place was always cold since they use an abundance of ice everywhere in the plant. Ice trucks had to be continuously unloaded as they pulled into the rear of the fish factory. Time went by well for Jack and he didn't mind the ten-hour work day. He tried to keep one foot ahead of Spencer, who was always checking up on him. Inspecting the buckets and table where Jack did his cutting, Spencer could find no fault with Jack's work. He had been at the factory over a week and did whatever he was ordered by Spencer. He was getting used to Spencer's argumentative attitude and felt that the name *Brute* fit him well. Jack was soon getting to be the best fillet man in the plant. By mid-afternoon, he had usually completed his work and thus had the rest of the day with Erin. They finally had enough money to survive in New York, and Jack started smoking a pack a day of the American cigarettes he loved so much. By the time he was there for a month, he felt as though things were looking up for him and Erin.

Erin was now in the fifth grade in the New York public school system and doing fine. Jack became friends with some of his coworkers, and after work, they would socialize and sometimes play cards. The Brute's name seemed to come up often and they discussed what a horrible man he was.

Peter Browne looked out his cottage kitchen window as he sipped his tea. Mae was at the stove baking fresh bread. Jack had been gone over a month now, and Peter was wondering why he had not heard from his brother. Jack had promised to write as soon as he found a flat and they had become settled. It started to rain, and Peter watched his boy Brendan playing with other boys in the empty lot across the way. The wind was kicking up and he wanted Brendan back home. Mae told him to leave the child alone, that he was fine. She also told Peter not to worry as Jack was fully capable of caring for himself and Erin. Nevertheless, Peter was concerned for the welfare of both of them. He couldn't write to them as he didn't have their address. If only he knew someone over there, it would surely make a difference. Several of the neighbors had made inquiries regarding Jack and his progress in America. All Peter could say was that he heard nothing yet. He took another sip of his tea, which was steaming, and told Mae he was going down to the boat to make sure it was secured as he thought there may be a storm coming.

As Peter left the house, Brendan saw him and ran toward his father. The boy was nine, and at times, he could be a terror. Like any nine-year-old, he was full of mischief and suspicious of everything happening around him. Peter sent him to retrieve another rope, which was down in the bottom of the cabin. Peter wanted to brace the boat so it wouldn't rupture if it knocked about. Once the boat was safely secured, Peter told his son they must get back home and out of the rain. As they were about to leave, they noticed Terrance Snow approaching them down an embankment. Peter asked him where he was going as there appeared to be a storm on the horizon.

Terrance said, "I saw you and Brendan down by the shore and I wanted to ask you if you had heard from your brother or Erin. It's been a while now since they left for America."

Peter told him there were no new developments since he last asked two days ago. All three started walking toward their homes. Terrance was a few years older than Brendan, but they were not really friends. Brendan had several close friends that he spent a lot of time with, but Terrance was more or less a loner.

Peter sat down at the supper table with his family and discussed the day's activities. He had a good day out on the sea and made himself some money. The fish was plentiful and he was thankful for that. Peter's daughter, who was eight and thus two years younger than Erin, sat at the table and asked for more milk. Brendan leaned over the table and gave her the pitcher.

Mae told her, "Drink all the milk you want as it will make you grow real fast."

Since Jack left, Peter hired two other men to assist him on his boat, but neither of them stayed on long, as they both proved unreliable. He had his own son Brendan out working with him a few times, but the boy hated the sea. Each time he stepped foot on the craft, he became seasick. Brendan didn't care much for the salt either, telling his mother it got all over his clothes. Peter then considered hiring Terrance Snow. He might be interested in making money to help his parents. His father didn't work and brought nothing into the household. He would have to teach the youngster the art of fishing and how to keep a boat afloat as well as cleaning and filleting the fish after it was caught. Mae didn't think it was such a good idea.

"It is so dangerous out there on the sea and so many things can go wrong. He is so young, just twelve, I believe. He returns to school next month. How is he going to work out on the sea and attend his classes?" Jack explained to Mae that children working during the daytime were allowed to make up their work at home. Some even went to the convent later in the day for their instructions.

By two in the morning, the wind was blowing so hard it sounded like the artillery in the Great War. Peter left his bed, looked out the kitchen window, and saw lights on in other homes. He knew his neighbors were concerned about the heavy wind and the damage it could do to these brittle dwellings. The storm continued during the night and into the following day. Peter could only hope his boat was safe. This was his livelihood. The storm did considerable damage to properties, blowing off several roofs. Some of the homes were washed into the sea during the horrific wind. There were nine deaths in all, including Mr. and Mrs. Snow. Young Terrance survived but was hospitalized in Neary, a few miles away. He had been injured when some of the debris from his house fell on him as he slept. His left arm was fractured and he suffered bruises to his nose and chin. He was one of the lucky ones as his injuries were not life threatening. He was released from the hospital after staying a week. The entire town of Downey Lock was in a morbid state.

Father McVey came to the hospital to comfort the boy during his stay. When he was informed of his parents' death, he took it so hard he had to be sedated. After his discharge from the hospital, Terrance was released into the custody of Father McVey. The priest told the boy he would be staying with him in the rectory until he could make arrangements for him to reside with relatives, if he had any. Terrance Snow didn't have any relatives willing to assist him. He was on his own from now on. There was a distant uncle on his mother's side, but he didn't want to get involved. The only thing left would be a state institution or a religious home. Father McVey looked into several of them.

There was St. Clair's in Dublin, which takes in stragglers and homeless children. Terrance didn't want to go to any home or orphanage. He asked Father McVey if he could stay with him, but it was against the diocese's rules and regulations. It looked bleak for the youth as the days wore on. Terrance was admitted to St. Joseph's Home for boys, an orphanage in Dublin, where he could remain until he turned sixteen. Peter attempted on several occasions to have Terrance placed closer to Downey Lock but was unsuccessful. Dean Massey wanted the boy to stay with him and his wife and their four children. One more in the family wouldn't matter. But because he was an owner of a pub, it wasn't allowed. Terrance was heartbroken, knowing he was leaving Downey Lock for an orphanage. Some of the people in the village took up a collection for him and, on the day of his departure, gave him home-baked cakes and other sweets. The boy was poor like most of the other people in the village but well liked.

Jack was doing fine with his new job and several weeks passed by without any problems. Erin was getting adjusted to her new school and making new friends. Jack wrote to his brother Peter but didn't mention in his letter the difficulties he met upon arriving. He told him of his new work and about his burdensome employer. At the fish house, Jack became rather friendly with another employee, Chris Matthews. Matthews was from Liverpool, England. He had been here in New York for several years now. Jack was still leery of being too close to a friend, as he didn't know him that well. But there was something about the man that made Jack comfortable when in his presence. He was tall like Jack and always seemed to be in a good mood. He was constantly making fun of the Brute and imitating him whenever possible. This always brought laughter to Jack and the rest of the employees.

7

Matthews had a brother who worked in Boston at the Boston dockyards. He was a longshoreman. The pay was good and they had a strong union that backed up the workers. Matthews told Jack on several occasions that he had the opportunity to work with his brother in Boston, but his wife refused to leave New York because she has many close relatives here in Manhattan. He told Jack there was not much fishing in Boston. But in the small town of Gloucester, which is north of Boston, they are always looking for fishermen. It is the largest fishing port on the Massachusetts seacoast. New Bedford is pretty big too, and it is the whaling port of the country. Jack was interested in all the news he could get about fishing.

Jack continued to work at the fish plant for almost a year under the Brute's authority and he didn't like it. The Brute knew that Jack could cut up more fish in an hour than two men. The Brute also had a penchant for constantly swearing at his employees whenever he became upset, calling them names that would make a sailor's face turn red. Louis Martel was on the shipping team that had to pack the fish in ice and get it out to the restaurants and stores. The Brute was always on this poor man for something. Martel was a small thin man who could not have weighed more than one hundred pounds. He had little education and depended on his fellow workers for assistance. At sixty-two, he moved slowly and was at times confused when attempting to understand orders. Spencer hated the little man and paid him less than the other workers. Martel was responsible for several jobs in the fishing plant. Besides packing fish, he also cleaned the toilets, mopped the floors, and followed any additional orders that Spencer dispensed. One late afternoon, Martel was scrubbing the floor in the delivery section of the plant. Spencer approached the little man and delivered a kick to the groin that knocked Martel to the concrete floor.

"How many times have I told you to put enough soap in the wash bucket? All you are doing is washing the floor with filthy water!"

Jack and the other men working nearby saw the entire altercation. Jack ran over to assist Martel, who at the moment was crying in pain. The Brute looked at both of them in disgust, shook his head, and left for his office without uttering a word. Jack did his best to comfort the injured man and sat him down on one of the chairs nearby. Two other workers also went over to assist Martel while Jack went into Spencer's office and started yelling at him, calling him a horrible person and hollering other obscenities. Spencer removed himself from his chair and was about to swing at Jack with his right hand when Jack landed a right cross squarely on his jaw. The blow stunned the Brute, and Jack landed a second punch to the midsection that bent Spencer over gagging and spitting up blood. A third right hand to the face knocked the Brute backward and out through one of the glass windows of the office. He was out cold as he lay on the floor.

"You may have killed him," whispered Chris Matthews.

Martel walked over to Jack and hugged him, thanking him for both his support and for punching out Spencer. The Brute was still on the floor but was now groaning. He lifted his head a little off the floor and told Jack he was done working at the plant. Furthermore, he threatened to file a police complaint against him. Martel immediately spoke up and presented the domineering boss with an ultimatum. If he did invoke the authorities against Jack, Martel was also going to file his own police complaint. Even better, he had several witnesses who would stand by him, and Spencer knew this too. Jack and Matthews went out to the front of the fish company to discuss what had just transpired.

"There's nothing here for you anymore, Jack. It would be best for you to get out of New York and make a fresh go of it somewhere else. Do you have enough money to make a change for you and Erin?"

"I'm fine," said Jack.

He didn't want to return to any more charitable organizations for assistance and handouts. It was then that Matthews presented an idea he thought might interest Jack.

"Why don't you go up to Boston and see my brother about working the docks?" As this was not something you jumped into, Jack had to have time to think. It would entail traveling to another state, which he knew absolutely nothing about. Erin had just become adjusted to her new surroundings and Jack knew she enjoyed her new school and classmates. She was also doing well in her studies. If they made another move, everything would change again and they knew no one in the city of Boston.

Matthews' brother Douglas had been working the docks for over ten years. He was a short man with a large stomach hanging over his belt. Fifty-seven years of age, but looked much older. A mostly pleasant fellow until you upset him. Douglas was married with seven children.

Matthews said, "If you decide to go to Boston, I will give you a letter, which I want you to deliver to my brother. I will give you his address and I will explain to him how you need work. Most days you will find him working the docks."

Jack and Erin alighted from the train and found themselves in Back Bay station in the center of Boston. Erin thought she was in another section of New York as the new surroundings appeared the same as the city she just left. It was a little after noon, so they decided to have a quick lunch and then see about accommodations. Jack wanted to see Douglas Matthews as soon as possible about working the docks. Although Chris Matthews didn't guarantee a job with his brother, Jack was still hopeful. It was now two thirty in the afternoon and Jack and Erin were just finishing their lunch in one of the restaurants on Boston Harbor. It was nothing special, just a small lunch shop. They both had the specialty of the day—franks and beans. Observing Erin's empty dish, one could see she enjoyed her meal. This was going to be another adventure, Jack told her. She was not to worry.

Erin told him she had dreamt of her mother again last night. She began to sob and then burst out crying onto the sleeve of her coat. Jack knew losing her mother at such a young age was horrific for his daughter. While at school in New York, she had to visit the school nurse on several occasions where she would break down in tears. Jack wondered if she was ever going to get over her sorrow.

They were able to obtain a small flat with a couple of rooms, which was more than substantial for them. The rent was more than adequate too. The following morning, Jack proceeded to the docks and made inquires to the whereabouts of Douglas Matthews. Several minutes later, as Jack was smoking a cigarette and standing close to some workers, he was approached by a short, stocky man.

"You looking for me?" asked the man.

Jack introduced himself and asked the man for a few minutes of his time. Matthews told Jack he was busy now with a new load coming off the boat, but instructed him to wait over on the next street. It may take thirty minutes, but no longer. He seemed to be a gentle, easy-going fellow.

After what seemed to be more like forty minutes and not the thirty he was promised, Jack continued to wait patiently for Douglas Matthews.

"So what is it that is so important that I am using up my break time?" asked Matthews.

Jack gave him the letter and stood by, saying nothing. Matthews read with enthusiasm and then said he had not heard from his brother Chris for some time now and wanted to know if he was well and how he was doing in Manhattan. Jack informed him that Chris was well and doing fine in the big city. Jack spotted a check in the envelope, which Douglas Matthews proceeded to read and return to the envelope. He noticed Matthews smiling as he read the check. No doubt, it was some money Chris had owed his older brother.

Matthews didn't have any fast connections to get Jack working on the docks. There were many people looking for work as longshoreman. But he did tell Jack he would talk to some of his friends who were in the union and in a position to possibly help him. But he made no promises to Jack. Sometimes people were employed part-time working the docks, and later would fill full-time positions. Whatever the content of the letter Chris Matthews wrote to his brother, it must have left an impression.

Douglas told Jack, "If my brother liked you, you must be a good fellow."

Douglas respected and had affection for his brother. Jack went to work the following day. For a couple of days each week, he worked a few hours in the morning. In the letter, Chris explained that Jack was a good person and had a daughter with him. He needed work as soon as possible and asked that he do whatever he could for him.

The ships that docked in the Boston Harbor came from mostly European countries. The cargo contained some of the most opulent furniture, machines, and other household goods. It was rugged and tough work with a boss constantly scrutinizing you and making sure you did your share of work. They wouldn't allow any indolence whatsoever, yet the pay was excellent. Jack was liked by his fellow workers, and his supervisors knew he was a willing employee. After a month, he was placed on full-time employment.

Boston had its share of speakeasies in comparison with Chicago and New York. They flourished in seedy neighborhoods, where the police were paid to look the other way. Longshoreman knew the exact location of these speakeasies. But Jack always kept the incident in New York, and it's far reaching implications, planted firmly at the back of his mind. The dockworkers were made up mostly of Italians, Portuguese, and some Polish with a handful of Irish individuals mixed in. Douglas Matthews had a son also working the docks. His name was Conlon. He was thirty and he and Jack became friendly rather quickly. They took their breaks and lunch together. He lived in the Back Bay section of Boston. He was married and had a daughter Ruth who was eleven years old, the same age as Erin. The girls never became close friends as Erin found her to be insipid. One girl was Irish and the other English. Ruth would at times make fun of Erin's Irish brogue and they would trade insults. At the time, there was a bad taste between the countries over matters of politics and religion.

That winter in Boston was cold and snowy. Jack and Erin moved to another third-floor flat closer to the docks, enabling Jack to walk to work. Jack started writing to Peter just about every five or six weeks. He told his brother he was getting along well and Erin was excelling in school. He deemed the food excellent and of good taste but acknowledged that some of the American dishes required some getting used to. The fish was of high quality but they used an awful lot of seasoning in its preparation. The fish and chips were much too greasy and couldn't compare with theirs in Ireland. Peter wrote in return and informed him of what had occurred with young Terrance. No one has heard from him since he was placed in the home.

When Terrance first arrived at St. Joseph's Home, he met Brother John O'Malley, a tall man in his early forties. He was a strong, powerful-looking person who rarely smiled. The institution was run by brothers, with an exception of a few priests. Brother O'Malley told Terrance what was expected of him and laid down the rules and regulations of the home. None were to be broken or discipline would follow. The brother asked him if he was hungry and led him into a small kitchen with a long table. He told the boy there were now sixty-seven children in the home, ranging in age from nine to sixteen. The brother made some toast and placed some jam on both slices. He poured a half a glass of milk for the boy and sat down next to him.

He said, "Let me explain to you, lad, this is a poor institution. We have little money coming in for support. So everyone who is here has to do their share. The children here don't want to be here, but there is nothing else for them."

Terrance was held spellbound by what the brother said. He talked with such authority but at the same time with a voice of compassion.

He continued by saying, "There are no walls or gates surrounding the home. Anyone can leave anytime they wish just by walking through the front door. We don't keep you a prisoner here. But if you decide to leave and go out on your own, there is no returning."

Terrance sipped his milk and ate his toast, saying nothing. The boy observed some of the paint falling off one of the sidewalls and a black spot on the ceiling that signaled where previous smoke damage had occurred. He reasoned that perhaps in the past there had been a fire on the stove. The toast felt good traveling down his stomach. Brother John sat back and rested in his chair to await some kind of response from the boy. The youth finally spoke and told the tall religious man he had no intentions of staying here, but rather planned to escape at first opportunity. He told the brother this was an orphanage and they were all the same. He heard of constant fighting, poor food when you could get it, and repeated beatings by the so-called caring nuns and priests. Brother John said, "We do our best here to eliminate heavy scolding. We have some very good football tournaments here and we play just about year round. Do you like the game of football?" The boy said nothing. He suggested the boy stay for a week here at St. Joseph's. He said, "If at that time you feel the same, we will attempt to place you somewhere else. I am not sure where that will be as there are not many options. You understand that don't you?" Terrance didn't say a word. He just sat there listening to Brother John and waiting for him to finish.

"Anyway it's time for you to see what goes on around here," added the brother. Terrance was given a tour of the home, and he was shown where he would be sleeping on the second floor. He was given three pairs of undershirts and shorts. Also, two pairs of knickers and four long stockings. There was a shed out on the grounds where some of the boys could take up woodworking. There was also a garden and paint shed. Terrance had no intention at all of staying at the home; he would be gone as soon as he got the chance. The brother told him to make friends and look over the place. He left Terrance and walked onto the grounds heading toward the shed.

The next day Terrance was sitting alone on one of the benches in the field when he noticed some kids playing football (soccer). He wasn't interested in any games right now. He hated the place and was depressed thinking about living there. He wondered how Erin was. Did she like living in America? She probably wanted to be back in Downey Lock. He thought of her every day and sometimes even dreamt of her at night. They were good dreams too. Somehow they were always down on the rocks near the sea or running through the fields. The picnics were so enjoyable. She would pack fruit and sandwiches for them both. He would always be upset if anyone came by and wanted to join them. Erin would always tell him not to be like that and to be friendly. He just didn't want anyone to spoil his fun with Erin.

After a few days, Terrance made friends with several other boys and was participating in his share of work. He would wash the stairs and help out in the kitchen as well. His bed was a little hard, but some of the kids told him they were all that way. Some of them made him laugh with their stories. One of the kids mentioned that the brothers were all strange. He had been here for over a year and still didn't trust any of them. One fourteen year old, Howard, told Terrance Brother John was the best brother. "He likes to look annoyed most of the time. I think that is so the rest of us will keep to our work and studies."

One afternoon, after being at the home for several days, Terrance walked to the rear of the main building and ran into Brother John, who was engaged in some work. There were several bags with some sort of powder in them. Brother John saw Terrance staring at the bags and said, "They contain cement, which makes concrete. Is that what you are wondering about?"

Terrance could see a large, unfinished hole apparently made by the brother. The boy was interested to know how big the hole would eventually be. "Grab the other shovel on the ground and help me dig this foundation," said the brother. Terrance didn't say anything but picked up the shovel and starting digging as he was told. The brother was a few feet away from him and continued digging too.

After working together for approximately ten minutes, Terrance asked, "What are we building?"

The brother said, "It's another building for storing supplies."

Terrance wanted to know why he was building it alone instead of employing professional builders. The brother told him he couldn't afford professional contractors to do the job.

He explained that "first, we dig the foundation. Then, we pour in the cement. We start at the bottom and build up." The brother pointed to a small shed adjacent to the administration building and stated, "I built that last semester."

They both continued to shovel while working up a sweat. He explained to Terrance that the home did not have any funds for supplemental construction by professional people. Anyways, he enjoyed helping out in this manner. They stopped and Brother John leaned on his shovel. With part of his white shirtsleeve, he wiped some sweat from his brow. He looked at the youth and saw him with a smile on his face.

Terrance also thought he recognized a change in the face of his coworker, but wasn't sure. Just for a minute was it a quirk or a smile. Terrance asked how big was the shed going to be. The brother walked over to a bench that had some tools on it and also a blueprint.

Brother John said, "Look at this blueprint, Terrance. It's nothing special and it won't be that large. It will be just big enough to house some gear, like soccer balls and other sports equipment."

The boy had never seen a blueprint before and asked the brother for some help in reading it. The brother leaned over the pattern, studied it for a moment, and then explained it to the interested young boy.

The trial week went by and Terrance was still at the home. Several more weeks passed and he was still there. Every day he was out assisting Brother John to build the shed. He was proud of what he was accomplishing with Brother John. It made him comfortable knowing he was doing something worthwhile. He also knew that Brother John was one of those individuals that wouldn't quit on a job until it was finished. The brother was a talented man who could probably build anything he wanted. So when Terrance wasn't in school or performing his scheduled chores inside of the main building, he was assisting Brother John.

The weeks turned into months and the boy learned how to survive inside of an orphanage. He also learned how to help other boys who couldn't care for themselves. Terrance was not a tough kid and he never looked for trouble, but when the occasion arose to defend himself against trouble-making youths, he never hesitated to elicit his bullish attitude. It wasn't long before the tall brother depended on Terrance to be on the grounds helping him with whatever he was doing. He became fond of the lad and his cheerful ways. The boy was never in a sad frame of mind. He looked up to the brother for solutions that he couldn't solve on his own. In no time, Terrance was laying other cement foundations and building other construction sites on the grounds of the home. He became an invaluable worker to the brother and an excellent reader of blueprints and other mechanical drawings despite never having any previous training in any of it. He learned just by observing and doing it on his own.

One afternoon right after school let out, Brother John asked Terrance if he had any plans for the rest of the day. When the boy said no, the brother said he was taking him to downtown Dublin for a movie. They took the train to the center of the big city and watched a Western film. Terrance knew this was something special since other kids at the home never were invited out like this. Later, they ate at a restaurant, both having corn beef and mashed potatoes. The brother ordered two glasses of Guinness.

"I suppose this is your first pint of Guinness, Terrance, am I correct?"

The boy smiled and replied, "No, in fact I had several of them when I was home in Downey Lock. Sometimes my father would leave some in his glass and I would finish it for him."

Terrance noticed a few sprinkles of raindrops hitting the side of the large window by the booth where they sat. There was a dimly lit hanging lantern overhead. The sky grew darker as they talked.

"Why didn't you become a priest? Why did you become a brother and not a priest?" asked Terrance.

"I never thought I was worthy enough to become a priest, said Brother John. "Anyway, I enjoy teaching and instructing children. Being here at the home for boys, I am able to help and give some hope to these kids. I can see it in their faces in the morning while they are eating breakfast. The little smiles and pleasure they receive while attending the outdoor soccer games. Some of the children believe that it is not that bad at the home. Perhaps, you might agree to that now, Terrance."

The boy sipped his beer and kept his eyes on his teacher without uttering a word. Brother John continued, "To be a Catholic priest, a person has to be in a certain frame of mind constantly and think about nothing else but serving God. I'm not that person. I debated it many times, but it wasn't for me."

Terrance said, "I think you would have been a great priest. However, I am glad you are here at St. Joseph's and that I met you."

The brother said it was time to leave and get back to the orphanage. The rain was coming down hard now, and being without umbrellas, they started running toward the train station, both laughing along the way.

8

On Erin's twelfth birthday, Jack took her to the Boston Commons where they had a picnic. Jack made sandwiches and brought some soft drinks along too. Just prior to leaving, he stopped off at a bakery and purchased two small cakes for both of them. The park was crowded with families, and being a nice mid-June day, there was not a cloud in the sky. Jack laid out a blanket under a tree and lit up a cigarette. He inhaled the smoke and then blew it out of his nose.

"Doesn't it hurt when it comes out of your nose like that?" asked Erin.

Jack laughed and shook his head and took another drag on the cigarette. It was a pleasure to be out on the grounds here with his daughter. Everything was going well for a change. He was making money and saving some too. Working the docks was hard work. It didn't matter because he loved getting up every morning early and seeing what another day would bring. He had Erin, his treasure, with him every day. While working a few days later, Jack was approached by Conlon and another man. Conlon introduced him to Jack and the trio became good friends. Conlon told Jack that Spike Travers had been working the docks since he was a young boy. He was now thirty-one. The three of them went everywhere together. After hearing some of Spike's stories about lifting some of the booze that came into the harbor early in the morning, Jack got the impression he was a sort of person who liked to live dangerously. Spike mentioned how shipments of liquor usually arrived after three in the morning. He told them of scotch, whiskeys, and other booze that they take off small boats in the harbor.

"We take them to shore and place the booze in trucks."

Conlon wanted to know how safe it was and what the chances were of getting nabbed. Spike told him they were far enough from the night shift workers at the main port that he saw no problem so far.

"I don't believe anyone has ever seen us lifting the booze. If they did, we never heard of any problems. I know smuggling booze is a federal crime with prison time if you're caught. I do not intend to ever be in that sort of situation. No jail for me," Spike said.

He told them the money was good, ten dollars for about an hour's work. He talked about them having their own security and lookouts.

There had been reports stated in the local newspapers regarding booze smuggling along the south and north shores of Massachusetts. There was one arrest made last month on Cape Cod. While Jack was working, Spike would talk to him about the new ideas he had about lifting some booze. Spike thought he might be able to get a truck after it was packed with whiskey and drive it to another city.

"Would you guys like to join in with me?" said Spike.

Spike wanted Jack and Conlon to understand he had been approached by one of the gang leaders to carry out some new job. He was to drive a truck to Springfield, Massachusetts, at three in the morning and park it in a certain location. There would be a car located for him a short distance away in which he would then return to Boston. He didn't even have to help unload the truck. He would receive twenty-five dollars for the entire trip. Neither Jack nor Conlon spoke while Spike revealed his new endeavor. "Twenty-five dollars is a large amount of money for a few hours' work. So would either of you be interested in working with me if I could arrange it? You have to understand that it is risky and dangerous. If apprehended, most likely you will be seeing the inside of a prison somewhere in the country. It's a serious and federal crime to be caught. Everybody wants to have a glass of whiskey or some booze in them."

Conlon spoke and related he didn't think prohibition would last long.

"People hate this law and it makes little sense!"

Jack stood fast and said nothing. He didn't like the danger in it. Just the thought of prison and leaving Erin was enough. But then again there was the money factor to consider. Twenty-five dollars a run could add up significantly.

"Hey, guys, just think about it and let me know later. Please don't mention this conversation to anyone," said Spike.

Later, while at a private club on the docks, Jack and Conlon went over their conversation with Spike. Jack wanted to know how many members were involved in this transaction. If there were too many people, it could become very dangerous. The more people, the more danger. People just can't keep their mouth shut.

Erin continued to do well in school. She found public school completely different than the Catholic private schools. The hours were a little shorter and there were no religious classes, which she missed. She often thought of her home in Downey Lock. She realized how completely different America was from Ireland. She would never forget those wonderful days when her mother was alive and well. The morning breakfast they always had together. She could see her mother and father in the kitchen now, talking away about something that occurred in the village, something crazy, which to her had no bearing on anything. They both would be puffing away on a cigarette and it would be dangling from their lips. Jack had not been with a woman since the death of Irene. It wasn't because Jack didn't have any interest, because he did. Jack was still a young man and he had the normal responses of a healthy male. Erin knew her father had not been in the company of a woman since her mother's death. Erin just thought her father had no interest because no woman could ever match up with his wife Irene. And she thought very little about her father's sexual desires.

Not far from the docks where Jack worked was a bus depot. After work, Jack would pass by this bus depot, and sitting in a ticket booth was a lady in her midthirties. Jack noticed her the first day he went by as she was attractive and had flaming red hair. There were times when there were people in line waiting their turn to purchase a bus ticket. But for the most part she was alone when Jack passed by. Jack, who rarely wore a hat, would pass by and wave if she was not busy. He wished at times he did have a hat on so he could tip his hat to her. One late afternoon, Jack saw her alone in the booth so he stopped and introduced himself.

"I have been passing by here and seeing you in this cage for many weeks and I just thought I would say hello. I'm Jack Browne . . . and that is *Browne* with an *e.*"

She replied, "Well I am glad you finally did stop and say hello, Mr. Jack Browne, with an *e.*"

They both laughed and she wanted to know where he was going each day about this time. Jack explained that it depended. There were times he was on his way home or going out to see a man about a horse.

"Well, I am Althea Monoski, and yes, I am Polish."

She knew what Jack meant by seeing a man about a horse since it was slang for a private club. It wasn't long before Jack and Althea were a twosome and seeing each other a couple of times a week. They enjoyed each other's company and liked being alone.

After leaving one of the private clubs that they frequented, they ended up at Jack's place. He told Althea his daughter would be in bed sleeping at this late hour. Erin was asleep when they entered Jack's apartment. Erin woke up as soon as the door opened and heard them giggling. Erin lay in her bed and listened to her father talking rather low and laughing every now and then. It surprised her to hear a woman with her father. She looked at the clock on the table and noticed it was 2:00 a.m. She heard her father say something about another drink for both of them. They continued to talk, but they were talking so low now she could hardly hear them. She couldn't distinguish the words they were saying. This really bothered her as she wanted to hear what the subject was and why the laughter. Then, there was nothing but quiet. She wondered if they left or if they were somewhere else in the apartment. There was only one other room and that was her father's bedroom. She thought she heard some mumbling, but she wasn't sure what was being spoken. She heard the woman call out Jack's name very slowly. Then, she again heard the woman call out her father's name. She heard her father's voice now. She couldn't understand what he was saying. She wanted to know what her father was doing with this woman in his bedroom. It now sounded like the woman was in agony as the strange woman was calling out her father's name more often. She was louder now. "Please, Jack, ohhhh." Jack was making some sort of noise himself that she never heard before. Erin wanted to get out of bed and run into the room and tell her father to stop hurting the woman. After several minutes, there was nothing but complete quiet in the apartment.

Erin lay in her bed frightened and confused. She heard them again, but now they had returned to the kitchen. She heard them talking so low she thought they were whispering. She thought perhaps she should go and talk to both of them and ask if everything was all right. They continued to talk softly in the kitchen. She heard the woman say to Jack that he was wonderful. She thought she heard her father laugh and then say something about Irishmen being passionate. A minute later, she heard the door close and there was silence in the apartment. Erin then realized both of them had just had sex. She felt they didn't make love because her father couldn't love a woman like that. Then perhaps he had forgotten his wife. She stared up at the ceiling and again thought of her mother. She tried to understand why her father would bring a woman into their home like he did. And she wondered how many times they did it in the past. Should she tell her father she knew about the woman? Perhaps it would be best to wait till the morning when she would be fully awake and had a clear head. She was concerned about her father's drinking. It was every day now and he was drinking more.

A few more months went by; Jack and Conlon decided to take up Spike's venture of making more money on the side. Spike was the middleman, and Jack and Conlon were to take care of what work they were given. It entailed loading and unloading trucks that were driven to different cities. Spike told them that if they were apprehended by the authorities, they were not to admit to anything. If they opened their mouths and ratted him or any other guy out, they would not live to see the following day. A few mornings later, both Jack and Conlon were on a work break when they were approached by two men they had never before seen. They were told plainly what would happen to them if they were caught and informed on anyone. They wondered who these two individuals were and how they fit into the entire scheme. Being threatened like this did not sit well with either of them. Twenty-five dollars extra a week was nothing to sneeze at. They both speculated as to where the locations were and how much driving was involved.

The following week they both teamed up and did their first job together. They drove to Worcester, which is thirty-five miles from the city of Boston. The week after that, Jack drove again to Worcester with another individual he didn't know. Scotch, whiskey, and other imported booze would be removed from small crafts, taken ashore, and loaded onto trucks that transported them across certain cities in the Greater New England area. There were times the truck's destinations were upstate New York and New Jersey. But for the most part, they made most of their drives in Massachusetts and Rhode Island. Providence was a pretty steady drive too. The boxes in the trucks were covered over with some sort of produce, usually lettuce. They never knew if they were driving with someone or if they would be alone. Jack liked working by himself and he kept a watchful eye along the way. He would see police cars on patrol or parked along the roadside, but he hadn't yet encountered a problem.

Since prohibition disturbed the drinking habits of many people, this was one of the ways they could still indulge. There was money to be made and Jack was going to get his share. Jack continued his day job on the docks and worked once or twice a week delivering booze. There were times he was busy weekends as well. Jack was saving his money and never spending it on foolish material things he didn't need. He dressed Erin well, and they moved to different flats when he thought it was in their best interest. He never liked staying too long in one particular place. He was always fearful of the authorities and what they might do if they found out about the work he had been doing on the side. He wasn't even a citizen yet. That was something he intended to do soon. He wanted it more for Erin than himself.

Many months went by but Jack never forgot his love for fishing. He wanted to make his living doing what he always loved. Everyone mentioned Gloucester when it came to the best fishing port, and the town was only a two-hour train ride from Boston. Anyone who had been at sea and had experience with nets would have no problem. This fit Jack perfectly.

On Erin's fourteenth birthday, they went to one of the nicest restaurants in the city of Boston. Jack told her that since he had been working extra hours on the docks he had been able to save more money. Jack had a large sum of money in the bank and he decided to move out of Boston. He wanted a place of his own like they had in Downey Lock. He believed he had enough money for a nice home by the ocean but that would require that he carry a monthly mortgage, as everyone else seemed to be doing. Since Gloucester is on the north shore, it was there that he decided to begin his search for their new home.

He had to get out of this booze business, never knowing when the law would come down on him. When he told Erin of his plans and asked her what she thought, she was not too pleased about moving again. She would have to make new friends all over again. Every day, people were complaining more and more about not being able to have a glass of wine at their dinner table. Jack believed that soon this crazy law would end and wine would be on everyone's dining room table again. Jack was happy to learn Erin decided to give him her blessing on looking for some land by the sea. It wouldn't have to be a large place since there were only the two of them. Jack resolved to start looking next month, in the spring.

The next day, when Jack reported to work on the docks, he was told one of their own was arrested last night, outside of Providence. He was caught with a truck full of gin and Scotch whiskeys. Conlon had spent the night in jail and was being held for the federal authorities. A Providence patrol car stopped him for no reason outside of being out at three in the morning. This frightened Jack so much that he couldn't keep up with his day's work and asked to go home. They excused him and Jack went directly home. He wondered if Conlon would implicate him or Spike and his friends. He was sick with worry. Conlon had been stopped about two years ago. He was able to talk his way out of it since they didn't find any alcohol. This was not good. This had to stop now. He had kept some of the money in his flat under a floorboard and had enough to get by. If he could land a job in Gloucester on one of those smaller boats, he would be in heaven. He went to the hallway closet, removed bottle of Irish whiskey, and poured himself a full glass. He looked outside the window and saw the rain pour down in sheets. What a miserable day this was.

Terrance woke at his usual time, close to 6:00 a.m. He hurriedly washed himself, dressed, brushed his teeth, and ran down into the kitchen. Brother John was at the table eating his oatmeal and sipping his tea.

"There isn't much we can do today about repairing the benches in the front of the main building," said Brother John.

They had intended to work on the benches that had been there for years and were falling apart. The top slots were loose and the paint was cracked and peeling. It had rained for six straight days with no signs of letting up.

Terrance could see that there was something bothering the brother. Terrance asked him if he was feeling well or if there was a problem with something. The brother assured him that he was fine, got up from the table, and left the kitchen. Terrance was one of the older boys at the institution. He had written to Peter Browne asking how Erin was and requesting her address in America. He never received a reply from Peter. He thought about her every day. She would be nearly fourteen now, and he would love to know where in America she lived. What Terrance didn't know was Peter received word from his brother Jack telling him not to give any information to the Snow boy. Jack had plenty of problems of his own and didn't need letters sent to his daughter from a kid in an orphanage.

Since Terrance was almost seventeen, Brother John informed him that the home was attempting to place him with a family somewhere in Dublin. He could hold his own and he was of working age. He was big for his age, so he shouldn't have a problem finding work. The home was overcrowded and short on beds. "It wasn't my idea, Terrance. The decision came from members of the committee in charge," explained the brother. Terrance had no intentions of living with a strange family. He would rather stay where he was. He believed he was better off here.

He told his friend, "If I have to leave, I will return to Downey Lock, not Dublin. I will get a room by myself and find a job. I won't accept any charity."

The brother told him it was reasonable to accept kindness. Don't be confused by the two.

"I was wondering if there were any problems waiting for you back in Downey Lock?" asked the brother. "Just remember to be kind to your friends and I am sure they will reciprocate. Kindness is a two-way street, and it flows best when there is not a traffic problem."

Brother John always made good sense when he talked one-on-one with an individual. Terrance thought how much he would miss this religious giant. He always felt at ease in his presence even though some of the children were scared of Brother John, who could be an intimidating person when he wanted to. Although he was slow to anger, he wasn't one to take lightly. When he spoke, his words were always completely heeded. Terrance always believed he was firm but fair.

Terrance retuned to Downey Lock and found shelter in a room over the Lion Heart. Dean Massey told Terrance he could keep the room as long as he helped in the pub. Massey had plans for the Lion Heart. He was putting on an addition to the building, and Terrance could assist the carpenter who was doing the work. Mr. Massey hired his brother from Dublin to construct the new addition. Besides enlarging the inside, he was installing inside plumbing. During the year, another pub had opened a quarter of a mile away. The Green Banner Pub was smaller than Massey's place, but it still had a good clientele. Downey Lock had grown some since Terrance's absence.

Walt Massey had been in the carpentry business since he was a boy. He knew how workers responded to this sort of work. They had to battle the weather and other elements that combined to make this one of the least chosen occupations. Outside work was not for everyone. Immediately after observing Terrance for a short time, Walter Massey knew he was a natural. The youth's enthusiasm and knowledge about his work was a joy for Walter. He liked the boy and thought his brother Dean had made a wise decision to keep him on. He knew his work and willingly accepted advice and new wisdom. He kept good track of his tools and kept them clean. Whoever taught this lad had done an excellent job.

It was summer now and the heat could be unbearable during the afternoon. Dean Massey would, later in the afternoon just prior to quitting time, bring his brother and Terrance cold mugs of beer. The two would sit down on a bench to sip their brew. Walter was interested in the kid and wanted to get to know him better. All he knew was that Terrance came from an orphanage, where he had been placed after his mother and father were killed during a storm. Terrance recounted for Walter all about his days in the orphanage and his experience learning under Brother John. Massey learned it was Brother John who taught Terrance the tricks of carpentry. Terrance expressed his fondness for the brother, giving him credit for bringing him along the straight and narrow path. He told Massey he trusted Brother John, for he was responsible for his new way of life.

Terrence continued, "I owe him everything. He taught me so much about life." He continued to speak of Brother John, not as a religious person, but as a good friend. Terrance said, "I don't believe I ever saw him pray. When he was in the chapel, he was always walking through or standing up. He'd be in the rear or side aisle with his arms folded. He was such an imposing person. I always thought he had a lot on his mind. I write to him regularly even though I've only received two letters in return." Massey listened intently as Terrance continued. "When I was in the orphanage, I was told Brother John had encountered some trouble in the northern part of the country. I believe it had something to do with politics." Terrance acknowledged that when someone speaks of an orphanage, it's always about the cruelty that occurs, but he clarified the misconception by saying, "I saw no beatings at anytime involving children. There was simple discipline, which you had to have when there are so many children together in close quarters. I learned to respect all the personnel who participated in caring for us." Every day, Massey would learn a new piece of information from his youthful friend, which was no tremendous feat given how Terrance liked to talk about his life. However, he didn't express much about his past when the subject of his parents arose. Everyone in Downey Lock knew the Snows and what happened to them. They were familiar with how the boy had suffered with difficult parents.

Terrance kept pestering Peter of the whereabouts of his brother and Erin and continued to request that Peter give him information on how he could write to Erin. Peter always had some excuse preventing Terrance from getting any direct information from him. Peter said only that the two were fine and on the move again. He did not know their new address.

Jack heard of a small village called Snugport several miles outside of Boston on the north shore. There was a large empty house with many bedrooms available. Jack worried that it might be too large for him and Erin, but then he decided he could rent out some rooms to assist with the mortgage. He made arrangements to visit the place. Assuming that she would be disappointed when she saw it, Jack did not bring Erin with him as he did not want to be biased by her opinion. Walking through the small town, Jack liked what he saw. He was impressed with the old Cape Cod houses. Along the shoreline, there were several foundations waiting to be constructed. He couldn't help but see the lighthouse not that far from shore and wondered if it was still in use, considering the many rocks in the surrounding area.

The "For Sale" sign in the front yard signaled that he had arrived at the house, which, he immediately noticed, had many windows. Jack counted five gables. The house appeared brown but was so dilapidated it was difficult to really tell what color it was. The shingles were peeling off, exposing the dry wood. He wasn't sure of the house, but he had to see the inside before he knew for sure. He certainly did not expect much, and he hoped it was safe inside.

Surprisingly, the interior was not that bad given that the house had been vacant for years. It needed some carpentry work along with some new plumbing, but nothing major. Jack himself had some past experience with electrical repairs. He thought he might be able to buy this house if the price could be lowered. He went outside and again checked the entire property to his satisfaction. He loved the way the house sat on its foundation so close to the ocean. The entire setting reminded him of Downey Lock and that alone made him certain that he wanted the property and everything that went with it, including its history. He was confident he could make this work for him and Erin, and he had enough money for the down payment. One of the central selling points was how much closer he would be to Gloucester. Jack thought it was good for him and Erin to get out of Boston. He explained to his friends and supervisors at work that he had other plans for the future.

9

Jack was able to get the property at a good price and planned to move in with Erin immediately. He needed to continue working, but he had enough funds to cover himself for a few weeks. He had made very good money running booze on the side. He banked all of it, knowing he would later need it. The day after he gave his notice to the personnel office, he went to Gloucester to see about working on one of those fishing vessels. He was surprised how easy it was to get hired. After applying for work in one of the employment offices and filling out the proper papers, he was assigned to work on a boat named the *Tug of War*.

Its skipper was a Portuguese man named Dante Ferrara. The boat carried a crew of five. Jack was interviewed by Ferrara regarding his experience in the fishing business. Ferrara told him he needed a good net man to assist the other crew members. After speaking with Jack for several minutes, he was impressed by what he said. Ferrara wanted to know if Jack had a drinking problem that would hinder his ability to function on a steady work schedule. Ferrara emphasized that they did not sit around the bay. They went out to sea and sometimes stayed overnight or even longer. The sea could be cruel and dangerous. In addition, Jack was asked if he was married and/or had children. Jack told him his wife had died and he was alone with his daughter. Finally, he asked Jack if he could start tomorrow morning. Jack replied he could and Ferrara told him to be at the *Tug of War* at 4:00 a.m. Jack was pleased with the salary, because it could be even more than what he received working on the docks in Boston. Jack had to take the 3:15 a.m. train where the nearest connection was to Gloucester.

Jack and Erin worked every day on their house. Jack usually returned home sometime around three in the afternoon. When the weather was unpleasant and the boats didn't move from port, Jack would help out the lobster men in the bay. This could be lucrative work as lobsters were always in demand. The months went by and Jack continued his fishing work in Gloucester. The next town over was Rockport. It was a heavy fishing village only a few miles away. In the center of Rockport, they had a restaurant well-known for steaks and roast beef dinners. Many of the fishermen from Gloucester and the surrounding towns frequented this restaurant, whose chef cooked them appetizing lobster dinners famous all over the north shore. The Ocean Front Restaurant had an excellent reputation not only for their food, but their service as well.

Jack told Erin he wanted to show her where he worked. It would be a nice train ride for her as she could take in some of the ocean sites along the way. He planned on taking her to the Ocean Front Restaurant for lunch later in the afternoon. Erin wore a new green-and-white dress she recently bought. She had on white socks and black shoes she polished specifically for the occasion. In her hair, she placed a green ribbon to match her dress.

Dante Ferrara resided in Gloucester with his wife Beatrice and his two children. They had a son, fourteen, and a daughter, eleven. He had owned the *Tug Of War* for over ten years, after buying it from another party who had it for five years. She was an old fishing boat, but she was kept in good repair by Ferrara. Anything the vessel needed the owner attended to immediately. The boat more than paid back its owner. Ferrara was able to make a good living fishing on the ocean.

While at the Ocean Front Restaurant, Jack saw his fishing master at one of the tables with one of the mates. Jack walked over to them and introduced his daughter. Jack was pleased that he was so well accepted by both of them. He enjoyed his small talk with both of them and then left to be seated at one of the tables. After their excellent lunch of beefsteaks and his favorite dessert, apple pie, Jack lit up a cigarette. He had black coffee to help digest his fine meal. Erin had left the table and was wandering around the rear of the restaurant. She was talking to another girl he had not seen before. She appeared to be the same age as Erin, perhaps a little younger. Suddenly, he felt someone's hand on the back of his shoulder. It was Dante Ferrara.

"Your daughter is talking to my Judy. How was your meal?"

Jack deemed it excellent. Ferrara explained to Jack how the sea can be a tough way to make a living.

He continued, "There are times I think about getting out of this racket and doing something else to make a living. It's such a dangerous way to go, really."

He took out his pipe and stuffed it with tobacco. He lit it and sat back in his chair. He could see how Jack loved the sea. It was in his blood.

"It's always been in mine too. I knew it since I was a young boy. I went to sea when I was twelve years old and have been fishing ever since."

Jack expressed that it had been the same for him as well. Here were two men enjoying what they do but sensing the danger of their work.

Jack liked his new skipper and thought highly of him. However, more importantly, he trusted him. Ferrara told him he had seen too many of his friends leave port and never return. Jack lit another cigarette and was about to order another soft drink when Ferrara nodded to the waiter. He told Jack to have something else for a change, and soon the waiter brought two glasses of whiskey. The skipper smiled and lit his pipe again and they both saluted each other. The hot whiskey felt good going down his esophagus and, even better, when it settled in his stomach. They continued on talking about the sea. The skipper told some of the different tales that occurred while out to sea. Jack said nothing for he did not want to interrupt him. He spoke of how one time one of his crew was lost at sea because of strange circumstances.

"We were out to sea perhaps ten miles when a storm came upon us. It wasn't a strong storm, but it was big enough to keep us busy. One of the crew, Alex Portivich, was about to go down to the cabin to get out of the wind, when we suddenly learned he was no longer on the boat. Two of the crew and I went looking for him, but couldn't find him. What we did find made us sick to our stomachs. He was apparently taken overboard by some sort of sea monster. We found part of his right arm on deck. It was torn from his body. Laying close by was some kind of fleshy part from a sea animal. I believed it came from a giant squid or octopus."

Jack was shocked by what he just heard. He knew there were stories of sea monsters and strange occurrences at sea. Jack asked if they found any other part of the man's body. "No," said the captain. The captain told of another story when the sea was calm and a crewman fell overboard with no explanation whatsoever. There were men on both sides of him. Yet neither of them saw him fall into the sea. Jack and his captain had another whiskey, and at this point in the conversation, Jack needed it badly. Jack wondered if the captain had one too many whiskeys as some of his tales were way out to sea, so to speak.

"The sea has so many strange stories one cannot remember them all," said the captain.

Jack just smiled and said, "Very interesting."

Erin and Judy came to the table to be with their fathers. Jack could see the love Ferrara's daughter had for her father. It made Jack feel good inside seeing Judy wrap her arms around her father's neck and stare up at him. Erin told Ferrara she loved the town of Gloucester and all the boats in port. She believed that his boat was by far the best looking of them all.

Since the death of Irene, Erin had been the cook in the house. Jack just did not like the idea of cooking. For one reason or another, he always had an excuse. He thought of it as rather feminine women's work. Jack did like to eat and he was rather fond of American food. The arrangement worked well as Erin loved to be in the kitchen making dinner for her father. She had mentioned more than once to her father the interest she had in attending a culinary school. While she was in Boston, she heard of the Molly Gardner Cooking School. If she was accepted into the school, she could take the train to Boston, which was not that long of a ride.

After that delicious lunch in Rockport with her father, she again asked him about attending the cooking school in Boston. Ultimately, she succeeded in persuading her father to allow her to attend the early summer session in late June. It was a twelve-week course, meeting three times a week during the day. She was overjoyed with being admitted and never missed a day. The summer hurried by, and soon, she was back to academics. Jack still had some work to do on the house, and he busied himself getting as much completed as possible before winter set in.

While at the school, she had the opportunity to learn the finer aspects of baking. The more she learned while on the job, the more certain she was that she could get a position cooking with some fine family if needed. She really enjoyed some of the Italian recipes she learned and was anxious to test them out on her father. He had already tasted her blueberry pie and thought it was grand. She stayed away from the Irish recipes she brought over from Ireland as she thought they were kind of bland compared to the new ones at the cooking school. That Sunday she made a Yankee Pot Roast, which was devoured by both of them. Jack attended Erin's graduation and, after tasting her numerous creations, knew he had made a smart investment in Erin's culinary school.

Erin had made some new friends at school and continued to be happy with her new surroundings. She often wondered why God worked the way he did. Why couldn't her mother be alive to enjoy this new life here? Of course, she knew it could have been worse if her father was not here with her. He never missed a day on the fishing boat. He worked long hours and he was tired by the time he arrived home. She wished he didn't drink so often and hoped he would quit smoking too. She had a feeling he was seeing a woman, perhaps from Gloucester or Rockport. He usually came home smelling of fish, but there were times when Erin swore she could smell perfume.

The one business this small town lacked was a bakery. Most of the bakery goods were brought in from Revere and Boston. United Food Supply was the town's only small grocery store. Harry Stedman was its proprietor, with his wife Stella helping out. They had no children. Word spread fast regarding Erin's talent with baked goods, and Mr. Stedman was willing to sell her pies. Soon after, he wanted her homemade breads. The ryes, sweet breads, and white bread were quick sellers. Between taking care of the house, school, and her father, she just didn't have the time to make all her bakery goods. She was a very busy young lady.

When Jack arrived at his boat, the sun was just starting to rise. It was a cool autumn morning with no breeze at all. Jack had lost count of how many times he and the *Tug of War* crew had been out to sea. The rest of the crew was already aboard. Captain Ferrara was smoking his pipe and discussing the weather with a member of his crew, Johnny Brannon.

When he saw Jack, he waved and called out to him, "You're late again, Jack."

Jack joked, "Not really, you're just early." They both laughed. Tommy Belcher was pumping fuel into the vessel.

He called out, "She's filled and ready to go."

There wasn't a cloud in the sky as the sun moved up. Jack thought to himself it was going to be one of those days that would be perfect for fishing. The boat slipped out of port as Jack noticed most of the other boats were still tied up. Several fishermen waved to them and wished them luck on their fishing. Soon they would be off too. The *Tug of War*, with her double engines running slowly, moved toward the sun and onto open waters. Captain Ferrara and his five shipmates were eager to reach their destination.

While at the dock, Peter's boat sprung a leak. It wasn't a bad leak and Peter was able to sustain it. But the trawler needed immediate attention. The leak was coming from one of the panels on the right side of the boat. Terrance soon learned of Peter's trouble, and later in the day, he went to where Peter's boat was tied up. He found Peter at the location assessing his problem. Terrance asked for permission to inspect the damage. Peter told him the wood panels were decaying from so many hours out on the sea.

"It will be months before she sails again," said Peter.

The trawler surely was in need of repairs, and Peter was looking at weeks, if not months, of costly repairs. This was not counting the money he would lose because of the delay.

"She doesn't have to be scrapped," said Terrance. "Order four bundles of three different size panels from Dublin. The other material we can get at the local general store."

Sunday was Terrance's day off from working on the new section of the pub. The pub was nearly finished, so Mr. Massey could complete the rest of the work himself. Terrance wanted to start immediately on Peter's boat. That Sunday, both Terrance and Peter gutted out the leaky section of the boat. With the new material, they worked night and day on the trawler, stopping only for a sip of hot tea and tea cakes. Peter would at times stop and stare at the young man in astonishment. Was this really the same boy who came from a decaying family and seemed to know nothing? Now he was a hardworking man, helping him to get his boat back onto the sea. It was amazing what Terrance could accomplish with his bare hands. He wasn't a boatbuilder, but his intuition guided him to complete even the most difficult task.

With the newly coated paint still drying, Peter intended to set sail shortly. After nine days, his boat was ready for the sea. Terrance refused any kind of payment. Peter was pleasantly surprised on the outcome of his boat. Throughout the entire time they worked together on Peter's boat, Terrance never once brought up the Brownes, thinking it would be best to wait till the trawler was repaired to bring up the subject. He thought by then he would have gained some influence and Peter might be ready to open up about his brother and Erin. Terrance ate regularly at Peter's home and never missed a dinner. It was at supper one night when Mae brought up Jack and Erin. She knew Terrance was anxious to hear about the pair. He stopped eating to listen attentively to every word Mae had to utter, but Peter's face showed an expression of frustration and disappointment.

"Oh, Peter, it is about time either you or I told Terrance the good news about Jack and Erin," said Mae. "She's well and she has asked about you in some of Jack's letters. Jack does the writing and speaks for Erin, although I believe we received two letters from Erin the entire time she has been gone. This I can say, Terrance, they both have had some problems along the way. They are now living in a small town not far from Boston," spoke Mae.

Peter interrupted and said, "They are indeed doing well. In fact, Jack has purchased a home for them in a town by the name of Snugport. I will give you more details later. I had promised Jack I wouldn't give out his address to anyone here in Downey Lock. I will write to him later in the week and explain to him how you would like to write to Erin. I am sure it will be fine with him by now. There shouldn't be any further problems with you knowing."

Terrance couldn't understand why Jack didn't want him to write to Erin. And what was the reason for such secrecy? Mae told Terrance of Erin's attendance at a cooking school in Boston and of how she had done well for herself selling baked goods in town. Jack had regular work on a vessel out of Gloucester. Both Mae and Peter wondered where Jack got the money to buy a house. Was it that easy to come by money in America? Terrance just sat and soaked up everything they said. He didn't want to miss a word, and when he wasn't sure about something, he would ask them for clarification. He still wondered if he would ever get their address in America. Why couldn't he keep in touch with them?

Peter brought out a bottle of ale and opened it. He poured three glasses for Mae, Terrance, and himself. Looking through the kitchen window, Terrance could see it was starting to rain and making its way in was the fog.

Peter said, "Drink, Terrance. Just relax and enjoy your drink. I know you're anxious to write to your friend."

The rain was pounding harder now, and Terrance was wondering if it rained as often in America as it did in Downey Lock where one could count on rain every day, even if just for a short time.

10

The *Tug of War* had now been out to sea for thirty hours. Everything was going well for the fishermen. Captain Ferrara noticed the sea was calm when they first left port. But now even the crew could see the waves weren't moving. Jack could tell Captain Ferrara was uneasy. In naval school, sailors were taught when the sea was calm, they were to be on guard as it signaled stormy weather ahead. The crew knew there was a storm brewing somewhere close by. An hour later, the skies became overcast. The rains followed. One of the crew suggested they head back to port. Captain Ferrara was no fool, and the one thing he didn't want to do was anger the crew. The ship was not full to capacity with fish, and to make the trip profitable, it needed to be full. Within the hour, the wind shifted from east to the south. Ferrara told one of the crewmen to keep a steady watch as they returned to Gloucester. Ferrara didn't like the change of wind blowing up the southern coast. Yet there wasn't any news coming from the wireless mentioning storms. The winds increased along with the rain and soon the weather was unbearable. It seemed as though the *Tug of War* was heading directly into the blow. Jack thought the wind was coming from every angle. Well versed in what had to be accomplished during any emergency, the crew tended to their duties as best as possible.

One of the crewmen shouted to Captain Ferrara, "She's taking on water down below!"

They needed to bail immediately. Jack was now at the wheel but was having a problem holding it still. The boat was rocking and he saw waves thirty feet high. Soon, they would be crashing down on him. The radioman couldn't receive or get through to anybody. No one responded to his constant shouts of Mayday. The boat continued to take on water against the catastrophic and unbearable wind.

At fourteen, Erin was more mature for her age than most. She had responsibilities now, not only taking care of her father, but her new house as well. Furthermore, she had to make sure her baked goods made it to the proper markets on time. There was an increase on orders from the neighbors too. With all of these obligations in addition to her schoolwork, she was utterly exhausted at the end of the day. But she was never as happy in life as she was now. She was excited when her father had a day off from fishing and they could be alone. The good times in Downey Lock would be discussed along with the bad. She loved reading some of the novels she was able to bring home from school, particularly stories of early America, as history was her favorite subject. It was her father who explained to her how America came to be the greatest nation in the world because the people worked hard. They stood by each other during both bad and good times.

Erin knew her father stopped off for drinks when the *Tug of War* returned to port in Gloucester. Sometimes he was too tired and would return immediately to sip his whiskey at his seaside home. Even when he stopped off, however, he was always home by six o'clock. Other thoughts raced through her mind. Was he lying on some saloon floor drunk? Did he get himself into a fight and end up in jail? She told herself she would wait up for him no matter how long it would take. When it was after midnight, Erin knew something was seriously wrong and she became scared. She hoped he wasn't injured. Where could he be?

That afternoon, Erin received word from some of the townpeople that there was a ship missing from Gloucester. It was late and it could not be reached on the wireless. She felt raindrops now and the shore became dark. She peered out toward the slowly blackening horizon. A storm was looming out at sea, and it was heading toward the shore. When Erin arrived in Gloucester, there were many questions about the ship and Captain Ferrara's crew. There were all kinds of questions being asked. Why didn't the fishing port have knowledge of the distant storm? Where was the captain's insight? The town of Gloucester and the people demanded an investigation. Most of the Boston papers expressed the same headlines, "Gloucester Fishing Boat Lost At Sea! Entire Crew Missing!"

Erin was devastated and stayed with one of the neighbors in Gloucester for the night. Everyone was aware of her devotion to her father, who himself was a well-respected man among the town's people. Erin refused any kind of food and asked only to be left alone. Food was the last thing on her mind right now. All she could think about was her vulnerable father in the vicious ocean, alone with the fish. Why was she being punished with the loss of the one person she loved more than life itself? Why now at a time when she needed him close by her? The manager of the hotel and several others thought it would be best if Erin was admitted to the local hospital for exhaustion and to have her mental state evaluated. She wasn't responding to questions and appeared to be incoherent. The next day she was discharged from the hospital. Her thoughts now were to return to her house by the sea. She wanted to be alone during her sorrow. The people in the town felt her grief and insisted on helping her.

There was a mass and a Christian burial for her father seven days after one of the crewmen washed up on the shore of Plymouth beach. His name was Tommy Bradshaw and he had been with Captain Ferrara since the *Tug of War* first went to sea. His was the only body recovered from the *Tug of War*. The coast guard and other ships went looking for debris or any other sorts of material left by the *Tug of War*. There was nothing left behind. She became another missing ship lost in a storm.

Erin was left alone in her house and she was slowly recovering her faculties. She sat on her bed and realized she had to depend on herself if she was to live in this world. She rose from the bed and looked from her bedroom window down toward the courtyard that surrounded the front of the house. There was no one else to approach for assistance. No close friends or family. Her uncle Peter was the only family she knew, but he was three thousand miles away in Ireland. She could return to Ireland but she quickly dismissed the idea from her mind. She would never go back to Downey Lock. It was her parent's dream of coming here and enjoying a new life. She wondered if she could make a go of it herself. How was she to make the payments for everything? The cost of living in this large house including the mortgage and other expenses would be enormous. She thought about selling the house and getting something smaller. Her father loved the house and it sat right on the ocean. The courtyard appeared lonely. The chairs on the porch were empty and everything seemed so depressing. Her father's favorite white rocking chair was still there. She could visualize him sitting in it, smoking one cigarette after another and sipping his best whiskey. She could see him walk to the rear of the house and peer out at the ocean. She knew he was happiest when he was home with her. He admired what he had accomplished in the short time he had been in America.

Erin decided to write a letter to her Uncle Peter to explain what happened to his brother. She resolved to get the letter out as soon as possible. She proceeded to a small desk in the corner of her father's room, where she remembered he kept all of his personal papers and letters from Ireland. She looked for Peter's address and any other written material that could be of assistance. She looked through a handful of letters and found one. She could hardly believe after all the time she lived in Downey Lock she couldn't remember Peter's home address. In any case, she wanted to be correct in her spelling. As she was returning the letters and other papers to their proper places, she noticed a large brown envelope in the rear of the drawer. When she opened it, she saw it contained several papers, one of which was a will made out by her father. There was another form that appeared to be related to an insurance policy. She looked it over but found it difficult to comprehend. She decided it would be best to check it out with an adult, but that adult had to be someone she could completely trust.

Mae opened the letter and stood by the kitchen window to read it. She continued to read as her eyes filled with tears. "Oh my God." It was now difficult for her to stand unsupported and she reached for something to hold on to. The first thing to enter her mind was how the young girl would be able to exist alone in America. Who would take care of Erin? She was alone without any support from anyone. Mae walked to the rear of the kitchen, looked out the window, and saw Peter and Terrance down by the seashore. She stepped outside and cried out Peter's name. Reflexively, Peter's first question was "what happened, Mae! Tell me!"

Peter and Terrance could see she was alarmed, and she appeared to be upset over the letter she was holding in her right hand. Peter took it from his wife and began to read it where he stood, right in the middle of the kitchen. Terrance was standing next to him with a face of despair. Peter sat down in one of the kitchen chairs, placed both hands over his face, and began to sob. Terrance picked the letter up from the table and read its contents.

When Mae was able to keep her emotions under control, she made some tea. All three sat at the kitchen table, heavy with grief. Peter and Mae discussed what they should do about their niece. They both wanted more details on how the boat sank.

Mae said, "We will write her and ask her to return to Downey Lock."

"Suppose she doesn't want to return?" asked Peter. "What then? She is fourteen now and has been in America for four years."

Mae acknowledged that Erin would have to sell the house.

"She will never be able to keep it now."

Terrance said nothing but listened intently to every word spoken between them. Terrance wanted to know what they meant about a house. Between the both of them, Peter and Mae filled Terrance in on everything they knew about Jack and Erin. They didn't know a whole lot because Jack was careful about what he included when he did write to Peter. Jack didn't want the people of Downey Lock to know any of his business, personal or otherwise.

"Did Erin ever write to you about me?" asked Terrance.

He glanced over at Peter, then Mae. Peter replied no, reminding them that Erin was alone in a foreign country and most likely in need of help. Terrance asked for more information regarding Erin.

"Please give me all the information you have on her, including her newest address," implored Terrance.

Peter nodded his head and complied. Later that day, Terrance wrote to Erin and told her how sorry he was to hear about the death of her father. He requested in the letter that she return to

Ireland as soon as possible, where she had friends and relatives who would look after her. Terrance was just turning seventeen years of age, yet talked like a man of unlimited knowledge. They had been separated now for over four years and he wondered if she ever thought about him. Why did she have to go to that stupid country anyway? Terrance thought the blame belonged entirely on Jack. He believed Erin didn't really want to go to America. She loved it here where she was born. She was an Ireland lassie and an Irish lassie she would always remain.

The next day, Peter saw Terrance in the village and stopped him. He told Terrance he had something for him, a small envelope he was carrying in his jacket pocket. Terrance opened it up slowly and inside was a picture of Erin taken earlier in the year. Peter walked away, leaving Terrance to keep staring at the picture. To Terrance, she appeared older than fourteen. The hair was darker, but perhaps that was due to the darker conditions in which the picture was taken. She wore a white blouse, which was slightly open in front. The skirt appeared to be black. She was so beautiful, thought Terrance. Her face was lovelier than ever. She still had the high cheekbones, but her hair was much longer and there were no ribbons or pins in it to distract you. She wore it naturally and had one of those smirks on her face one typically wore when embarrassed. Only on her could it be cute. To select one best feature of this young beauty would prove an impossible task. Even her nose and mouth were perfect, with her teeth even and ever so bright.

Peter approached Terrance and told him he wanted to speak to him about Erin. Peter explained he wasn't sure what Erin's plans were regarding returning to Downey Lock. He went on, "There is nothing any of us can do if she refuses to come back." Peter wanted to know exactly what Terrance's feeling and intentions were toward his niece.

"Is it some sort of childhood emotion or is it more, Terrance?" asked Peter.

"There is nothing immature about my emotions for Erin," replied Terrance.

"She was ten years old the last time you saw her. She is living her own life now. Please be practical about this. She doesn't even know if you're still alive. If she does return, leave her alone and go your own way," said Peter.

Terrance was surprised by the way Peter was acting and shocked at his attempts to sway him away from Erin.

People in town started talking about the girl in the big house. Her father probably had no form of insurance to help support Erin. Clyde Farrow had been the mayor of Snugport for twelve years. He was a portly man and partly bald. He was well respected, but had his share of critics among the townspeople. He would always stop you on the street to say hello, but his chatter mouth could easily tie you up and you would lose those precious minutes you needed. He was seldom in the town hall as he was too busy walking the downtown area talking his mouth off. He was always complaining about his health even though most people confirmed he was as healthy as a horse. If it was not his health, it was some other foolish matter. This irritated the townspeople. But today, people were stopping him on the street, for they wanted to know what he had in mind for the young girl who was underage and living alone in the house by the ocean. The majority were concerned about her welfare. It had been a week now, and they were convinced that nothing of any good would come of this situation. A meeting was planned for Friday evening at the town library right after supper.

11

Dorothy Sinclare was the head librarian. She was single and, at age forty-two, very independent. Some newcomers to the town thought she was the mayor since she was always in control of everything. If you wanted something done, she was the person to see. She headed most of the projects in town and knew the personal history of every resident. She was small, of average weight, had brown hair, wore no jewelry, and had black-rimmed glasses perched on the bridge of her nose. She had rather large eyes, visible when she removed her glasses. Seventeen people showed up for the meeting including Dorothy Sinclare. It was decided she would be in charge given that the meeting was being held at her place of employment. In attendance were ten women and seven men. Ms. Sinclare made the opening remarks, claiming that Erin Browne refused to leave her home and wanted to continue living at her residence. She refused to attend the meeting, saying she already knew that the people wanted her to leave her home because of her age.

A gentleman was sitting close by where Ms. Sinclare was speaking. He was new in town and only Ms. Sinclare knew who he was. His name was Connor Newton, from Boston. Ms.

Sinclare contacted him specifically for assistance in this matter. He was a social worker from Family Services. He sat and listened to the group speak, never interrupting. Everyone present only wanted the best for Erin, but her being alone in that huge house was completely out of the question. After approximately twenty minutes of discussing Erin's situation, Ms. Sinclare introduced Mr. Newton. Newton informed everyone attending that they were correct; the young girl could not be allowed to stay alone. Ms. Sinclare interrupted and told everyone that Erin would probably lose the house in the near future as she would never be able to meet the payments and the accompanying responsibilities.

"Was there any insurance left for the child?" asked Newton.

"Nothing. Her father was a fisherman from Gloucester. How he was able to buy this house in the first place is beyond us all," said Ms. Sinclare.

"What about deportation? She is not a citizen of this country. Neither was her father. What grounds do we have on this matter?" asked the library official.

Newton replied he was not sure of the law regarding this sort of situation but reiterated that "this girl has not done anything to be expelled from this country. She is alone and needs help. Her father is dead. Whether he was a citizen doesn't come into the picture now. Our focus now is Erin Browne."

The meeting continued another hour with nothing accomplished.

"I will see if we can place her in an institution when I report to work tomorrow morning," said Newton.

Ms. Sinclare didn't believe the girl should be allowed another night on her own. All agreed her living alone was dangerous. The front door opened and Mr. and Mrs. Stedman walked into the room. They excused themselves for being late and were briefed on what had occurred. Stella related to the people there that she and her husband would like to take Erin in and be responsible for her. She told everyone there was no reason to place the adolescent into a home.

"My husband and I will talk to Erin tonight as soon as we leave here."

Several of the participants expressed joy after hearing what the Stedman's said. They thought they had finally achieved a solution to this ordeal. It made most of them happy. The librarian, however, was not satisfied with this arrangement and said she was not so sure this was the end of the problem. The Stedmans were pleased with the outcome and saw no issue with Erin accepting their invitation. Sinclare was afraid of what other towns would say if there was a disaster with Erin. She didn't think the town should put themselves in such a precarious position.

The Stedmans found Erin in the courtyard in front of the house looking over some papers. Erin was pleased to see them and welcomed them both. Stella told Erin of the meeting that was just held about her and what they suggested doing to eliminate any further problems. She was asked by Mrs. Stedman if she would be willing to stay with them during the evening hours and sleep at their house. She would be under the care of the Stedmans until she reached the age of eighteen. They would all have to get permission from the family court system.

This way, Erin would be able to still take care of her house and be under adult supervision too. It was either this or be taken away to a state institution till the age of eighteen. Erin didn't want anything to do with being away from her own house or her school so she was extremely grateful for the couple's offer. She told them how much she appreciated their help and agreed to their proposal, promising to help them any way she could. She would never be a problem for them. She thought now may be a good time to mention what she discovered in her father's room but wrestled with the decision. Then she thought perhaps this wasn't the best time. She trusted the Stedmans but didn't really know them personally. Erin did like the idea of staying with the Stedmans and wanted everything to work out for all involved, but if it didn't, she resolved to leave and find some other supervision that would allow her to stay with her house.

The next day at school, she went to the principal's office and spoke with Mr. Carl Ferland, the school principal. Ferland had been an educator for twenty years. He was a short man with a thin built, wore a medium mustache, and was usually a pleasant person. He was well liked by both teachers and students. Ferland, like most of the people in town, knew of Erin's loss and was very sympathetic. She told him of the papers she had found regarding her father, the will and insurance policy. She asked that he look them over as she didn't understand some of the writing. He told her he was not an expert either but would inspect them for her as best he could. They sat at Ferland's desk, where the principal read for approximately ten minutes and then placed the papers down on his desk. He told her to wait here for a minute and left his office. He returned minutes later with another teacher, Ellen Bureau, who was the English teacher at the school. Mrs. Bureau worked in an insurance company before becoming a schoolteacher. Mrs. Bureau read over both the will and insurance policy and explained to Erin that it was imperative that she see an attorney immediately. She could be coming into a great amount of money.

"The way I digest this will, Erin, upon his death, your father left you everything, including the house, everything in it and everything he owned. It all belongs to you. I don't see any other name mentioned in the will. The insurance policy states, if I am reading it correctly, you are to receive the amount of $5,000. A hefty sum I must admit," she said, smiling at Erin.

Ferland burst out laughing and patted Erin on the shoulder. "Wonderful!" he exclaimed.

Mrs. Bureau added, "Of course, I am not a lawyer and you should see one as soon as possible."

Erin thanked them for their help and assured the both of them that she would do as they suggested.

Erin decided to go to Boston to seek out an attorney. She was given a name of an attorney by the principal, but wanted to go on her own to someone who was well established. She informed the Stedmans she would be moving in that day and would close up her house for the time being. She then told them of what she had discovered and explained that she had to see an attorney as soon as she could. She asked them if one or both of them could make the trip to Boston with her. The Stedmans asked to see the will and insurance policy and were pleased after reading them. They both seemed very happy for the girl. Mr. Stedman said he would be willing to go with her to Boston and select a reputable lawyer.

"Of course, we have our own lawyer and he has assisted us for years. He is right here in town and we could go to him if you wish," said Mr.Stedman.

"I want to go to the lawyer my father went to. I believe he is in Boston," said Erin. "I recall my father saying that the best and smartest lawyers are in Boston."

Mr. Stedman replied, "Of course we will, and we shall leave tomorrow morning." Stella then asked Erin to come with her. She wanted to show Erin her room.

It wasn't that difficult to find the attorney who represented her father. Phillip Hastings remembered her father and was surprised to learn he had died at sea. Hastings was a huge man in his fifties, clean shaven, with a reddish face. He appeared to spend most of his time at the dinner table and was probably not one to refuse an alcoholic beverage if he could find one during these times of prohibition. But with the correct connection, one could find alcohol if they wanted to. It was now one of those laws that were frequently misunderstood and which most people wanted abolished. Hastings explained the executive of the will was a man named Howard Benson, a friend of Jack. "It would be nice if he could be found before this matter is brought to probate court," explained Hastings.

Hastings examined the will, checked on the insurance policy, and looked over at Erin with a smile. Erin asked him if it was true, if her father left her five thousand dollars when he was lost at sea.

"No," replied Hastings. "That is not true. In fact, because of his accidental death at sea, caused by a hurricane, the sum doubles. Erin, you will receive ten thousand dollars. If it was a normal death, heart disease or cancer for example, then only the normal amount would be paid out. A fisherman's occupation is a dangerous one. Your father was a nice man. I was first introduced to him by Howard Benson, another fisherman who I haven't seen in many years."

Erin was stunned by the news of receiving such a large sum of money. She was completely overwhelmed. She removed a handkerchief from her handbag and began to sob. Hastings stated she wouldn't see any of the money until she reached eighteen. That was the way her father wanted it in the will. At that time, she would be at a responsible age, and since the house would be paid off immediately after her father's death, she would always have a place to live. Her father knew exactly what he wanted for his daughter and made sure she would always be taken care of, even when he wasn't present. In closing Hastings said, if there was anything she needed, she was to contact him immediately. If there was a need of money for repairs on the house, he would be able to make funds available to her. Hastings told Mr. Stedman there would be provisions for him also. He and his wife weren't expected to be responsible for all of the expenses for keeping Erin. Of course, all of this had to be agreed upon in probate court. Hastings foresaw no problem with these arrangements in the court system.

Now that she was living with the Stedmans, Erin found her life changed completely. She yearned to be on her own. She appreciated what her new foster parents were doing for her, but she wanted to be back at her house and in her own bedroom. She barely knew these people and now she was living with them. She found them to be a kind and very thoughtful couple. Since they had no children of their own, they were extremely happy that Erin was now directly in their lives. Every chance Erin got, she went back to her home by the sea. The death of her father never left her. It was with her every day.

The Stedmans watched over her closely. They didn't attempt to interfere with her decisions, but were there for her with their advice if asked. It wasn't that easy for Erin to adjust to the new surroundings. She spent many hours alone in her room reading. She loved to be at her beach and feel the sand under her feet. She wondered why she felt so comfortable when she was alone. In her mind, she could see her father running along the surf as he often did. How he would wave at her when he saw her in the backyard. He ran as much as he could, as he enjoyed exercising. He believed running in the waves that came ashore only strengthened his legs. Ironically, he usually had a cigarette dangling from his lips while he jogged.

12

Four years passed quickly for Erin. She couldn't wait to be on her own and live alone in her house. It wasn't that she didn't like living with the Stedmans, one could not have had better foster parents. She was accepted by them and treated as well as anyone could be under such conditions. At seventeen, she graduated from the local high school with honors. She continued cooking and selling her baked goods. When she was old enough, she purchased a Ford Station Wagon for her deliveries. The Stedmans would always be in her thoughts, and she knew she could always depend on them for support and advice in the future. Erin was now corresponding regularly with Terrance and was kept abreast of what was occurring in Downey Lock. Peter also kept in touch with Erin and wrote to her monthly from the green country.

Terrance was doing mostly carpentry work in Dublin and staying in one of the less expensive hotels on McConnell Street. He was now twenty and well versed in the carpentry trade. He enjoyed his occupation and was a conscientious tradesman. He was in demand because of his craftsmanship and his fine attention to detail. It was no longer on-the-job training for him. There were very few jobs he could not complete. Terrance saved most of his earnings, keeping just enough for him to subsist on. He had his own bank account and enjoyed seeing it rise every month. He wanted to visit Erin in America. He thought if he had two hundred dollars saved, that would suffice until he could find work. But he worried how Erin would respond to him after so many years apart. In her letters, she never mentioned him coming to visit her. She was a big girl now and on her own. She had her own friends and probably a boyfriend. She had her own house and was able to make a go of it with her cooking. Did she want an ignorant foreigner in her way now that she was successful? He thought of surprising her and then realized it wasn't a good idea. She probably would not like anyone imposing on her. It would be best if he wrote and informed her he was coming to visit for a short time. That way, if his visit was a mistake, he would soon know it and could leave when he wanted to.

He decided to write asking whether the conditions were right for him to visit her at this time. It was now winter; he thought it would be best to wait until spring to go if she accepted his request to visit. He anxiously waited to see her again. He wondered what her house would look like. She had mentioned repairs needed around the house and he couldn't help thinking that they would no longer be a problem if she accepted his visit. After such rumination, Terrance decided not to think about things that may never occur.

Erin wanted to become a citizen and started investigating what she had to do to become one. She would start studying and go to the library to get all the facts from Ms. Sinclare. She was so happy when she passed all the tests and became a citizen. Yet she loved to think back to the days in Ireland during her early childhood; they were happy days. Like the time she and Terrance went to the caves at the seashore. The caverns were so black inside no one could see anything. She remembered her father telling her the caves spread underground all the way through Downey Lock and farther. Terrance loved to explore the unknown and had no fear of dangerous locations.

"Don't be afraid, Erin," assured Terrance.

He would hold her hand while they continued their walk underground. He would light a torch made out of dried seaweed and wheat straw and this would illuminate the darkness. The two of them spent many hours exploring the many caves. Erin was amazed how Terrance could find his way around the caves; it was like he had direct knowledge of the all the entrances and exits.

Many times, however, Terrance would scare her and pretend he couldn't find his way out and they were lost. He would warn her of a monster leering somewhere ahead, at which point she would hold his hand tighter and let out a gasp of excitement. She loved the way he laughed and told her not to worry. "Your prince is here to protect you. I will protect you from any ghost or evildoers in the world!" He had a way about blowing out the torch and having it light up again, like some kind of illusionist.

Although they explored most of the caverns, there still were many they hadn't visited. There were times she noticed he was a very private individual. It was not that he was moody or standoffish, just that he wanted to be alone at particular times. He was also kind and thoughtful. She knew most of the other children in Ireland laughed at him behind his back, but none did so to his face as he was much taller and stronger than most. In the entire time she was in Downey Lock, she only saw him in one fight and the other boy took a beating. If she remembered correctly, they fought over her, after the other boy made an off-color remark about her in the school playground. Children made terrible remarks about his parents and the clothes he wore, yet he never held a grudge against any of the lads who abused him with their words. She knew the only friend he had was her and she kind of liked it that way. She wondered what he would look like at twenty. Would he still be handsome and strong looking? Would he still possess that quality appearance that made him stand out? The last time she saw him, he was twelve but sometimes, people change for the worst.

The Chapinwick Country Club was a private establishment located right outside of Snugport. The club consisted mainly of wealthy members. It was your typical country club with golf, tennis, and a large swimming pool. To belong, one had to be screened by a security panel. The annual fee was a hefty price that kept some people from applying. There was a five-year waiting list as only a certain amount of members were allowed. This way, members would not be waiting hours for tee time on the course. Like many private country clubs, it had a snobbish background. The food was exquisite and only the best chefs were engaged.

Jarvis Mandeville and his family were members. His wife Freda and two sons, Albert and Andrew, were also members. Jarvis and his wife were both French Canadian. He was in the textile business and owned a weaving mill a few miles outside of Snugport. His business was doing fine as he had many government contracts.

Albert had just graduated from one of the most prestigious universities in the Boston area, whereas Andrew was studying at a college in Worcester. The two sons were expected to enter right into the textile business with their father. It was the end of January on a Friday evening and it was pouring rain, a miserable night for a celebration. There were over a hundred people attending Albert's graduation party. Many of the town leaders as well as personal friends of Jarvis Mandeville were present. Albert was of average height, on the thin side. At twenty-two, he was a rather handsome fellow, despite having one ear a little larger than the other. He also had a small nose, which gave his smile a pleasant appearance. A likeable individual, Albert had many friends in the Snugport and Salem area.

Erin had earned the fine reputation of having the best-baked goods in the area. She was responsible for baking the pies and cakes for the country club. Since she now had her driving license and her station wagon, she made her own deliveries to the club, but there were times she would have to go to the club and bake some of her pastry in their ovens, especially if there was a large party. Erin left the kitchen through the swinging doors, stopped, and looked out into the dining room. The room was filled to capacity. Everyone was eating and having a good time. Some of these people she had seen on the streets of Snugport and Salem. Immediately, she realized she was not in the same category as them. They were not only snobbish, but obnoxious too. They looked down on the common people; she saw the same kind in Downey Lock. But then she thought of how nice and comfortable it would be to belong to society. At one of the tables was a group of five. One of the individuals left the table and passed Erin on his way to the kitchen. He immediately turned around, then proceeded through the swinging doors, stopped in front of Erin, and asked who she was.

"My name is Erin Browne," she replied.

With a large smile on his face, he introduced himself. He told her his name was Albert Mandeville. Erin was wearing a white apron wrapped round her waist.

"You are the most beautiful young woman here. Do you realize that?" asked Albert. "You have the face of an angel," he told her.

He continued to keep his smiling face looking directly at Erin.

"I work here and I am glad to meet you too Mr. Mandeville," said Erin.

"Please Al is what all my friends call me. Where have you been hiding, Erin?" Erin told him she was the pastry baker and was here because she had some work to complete. They were suddenly interrupted by Jarvis Mandeville. He placed his hand on his son's shoulder and asked him to return to his table. Albert told his father he would be back later but his father insisted he return to the table now.

"In a few minutes, Father, I won't be long. Go back with Mother," he said as he kept his eyes on the young girl in front of him.

It was like he feared she would disappear on him and he would never see her again. His father left, not too pleased with the outcome.

"So are you the one who makes those delicious blueberry pies and other goodies?" he said as he continued to smile at her. "Your baking is terrific. I was on my way to the kitchen to see what looked tempting just before I saw you standing there alone. I get along well with the kitchen help and the chefs," said Albert. Erin thanked him. Albert asked her if she was finished working for the evening. She told him she was and would be leaving soon. Albert took her hand and asked her to follow him. They hurried down a long hallway then down two flights of stairs to the cellar. They approached a room with many people and several candles lit. There was a bar full of men and several women in attendance. All were drinking and partying and having a grand time. Albert told Erin to wait a moment, that he would get drinks for them. She heard of these places where people could consume alcohol without being concerned about the police. Prohibition was still going strong and being enforced in the country. Albert came back with two glasses of booze and they sat at a table together. "Cheers!" he said to Erin as they touched glasses and swallowed their drinks.

Albert could see Erin was having a difficult time drinking her whiskey. She made a face and Albert knew she was not enjoying her drink. She told him "I really am just a beer drinker. I am not used to strong whiskey." He left and came back with a large glass of beer. He wanted to know everything regarding the young girl sitting next to him. He asked who she was seeing, if anyone. Erin wasn't about to tell this stranger her entire life story, but she had some interest in him. He didn't appear to be one of those snobbish fools from the private club.

She told him she lost her father to the sea and now lived alone in Snugport, and no, she wasn't seeing anyone special at the present time. She didn't date because she didn't have the time. Her house and her baking kept her busy. He didn't question her on any of her answers and stopped talking when he thought she was getting a little tired. She liked his smile and his face was delightful. His brown eyes appeared kind and, at the same time, sad. His hair was blondish, combed back, and parted to the side. She deemed him a bright and exciting young man. He told her everything regarding his life that he could remember. He tried not to leave out any details. On several occasions, she interrupted him and asked about his university days and what he planned to do with his life. He told her he dated frequently almost every weekend if he wasn't out with his friends. Inside, Albert was thinking of how he had never seen a girl like Erin before. Her beauty was striking and he was devouring it.

"I am very sorry to hear about the death of your father. He was a fisherman if I remember correctly. Since you have been a kid, you made it on your own. I recall my parents talking about you. How old are you now?" he asked.

"Eighteen," she replied.

Albert was impressed with all Erin revealed. She got up from the table and thanked him for her beer and told him it was getting late. She had to leave now. They were interrupted by Albert's father telling him he was needed upstairs.

"May I call on you in the near future?" asked Albert.

But Erin had already left his presence and didn't hear his closing remarks. Albert's father was furious. "What the hell is the matter with you bringing that girl down here with all these prestigious guests and members indulging in alcohol? Get back upstairs to your table." Albert had lost his prodigious smile and walked away from his father to the bar where he ordered another whiskey.

13

Erin received four letters from Terrance during the next month. He was writing more than ever. She was wondering where he found all the time to write. She was happy to read in his letters that he enjoyed and was a success at his occupation. He never expressed his feelings for her. They were simply letters that a friend would write to another friend. At the end of each letter, he would sign, "Your friend, Terrance." She mentioned on at least two occasions that her house needed repairs, but he never responded back in the affirmative saying someday he would come there and help her with those repairs. Erin thought she should write something in her next letter and invite Terrance to take a holiday to see what America looks like. She didn't need him to work on her property because she had enough money of her own to pay for those services. She thought of how pleasant it would be to see him again and she would enjoy his company.

It took Albert Mandeville two days to get up the courage to call on the baker in the large house next to the sea. The Crystal Manor, located on the outskirts of Salem, had an impeccable reputation for their food and service. Only the wealthy frequented this eatery and one could expect to have a fine meal prepared for them with soft music playing in the background. Erin was impressed with the Crystal Manor's elegance and with the handsome man across from her. Albert had a certain amount of charm about him and knew all the right words to express his affections to his new girlfriend.

This was really Erin's first date. Those occasional nights out with the kids from high school were just children's outings, not something as serious as this encounter with fine company. Albert was surprised by how knowledgeable she was. She never missed a beat when discussing politics and situations in the world. She was eighteen going on twenty-eight. She was reserved when she talked but never broke eye contact. She would never be accepted by his family. She would never be affluent enough for them. They knew her background and thought of her only as a commoner with no nobility. Albert didn't care what his parents thought about Erin for he had his own ideas and values. This young maiden held a grip on him.

She wasn't like most girls he dated. He had every intention to go slow with her and not to rush her. They had a pleasant evening dining and later went to a coffee shop. Albert continued talking about going into his father's business. There was talk about a possible recession, and some mills and manufacturers were uneasy about new orders. Some businesses were slowing down, but Albert said his father's business was going strong with new orders from the government. He told Erin his father promised him a new automobile if he came to work immediately.

It was close to eleven o'clock when he brought Erin to her house. She thanked him for a nice evening and patted him on the shoulder. There was no good night kiss. Albert decided there would be plenty of time for kisses later. But on his way home, he thought about holding Erin in his arms and kissing her lips. The following day Erin ran through memories of the preceding night in her mind. She liked him and thought him to be a gentleman. She went for the mail and there was a letter from Terrance among some bills that had to be paid. The letter told of Terrance coming over to Boston. He mentioned in his letter that a construction firm had answered his application regarding work. He explained his expertise and they appeared anxious to hire him for some of their projects. She smiled when it came to the part about him coming to Boston and thought it would be nice to finally see him again.

The next morning Erin visited the Stedmans at their store. It was snowing and late February could be the coldest month of the winter season. She told the Stedmans about her first evening out with Albert Mandeville. She asked her dearest friends for their opinion about dating Albert Mandeville. Stella told her there was not much she could say about Albert. He came from one of the most prominent families on the north shore of Boston. There wasn't any serious gossip she knew of and he kept out of trouble for the most part.

"He grew up rich, but one can't hold that against him," said Mr. Stedman.

In turn, they asked how she was making out now that she was on her own.

"Fine," she replied.

Throughout the course of her four-year stay with the Stedmans, she told them of her entire life story, including her good friend Terrance Snow. Today, she mentioned to them that he was considering coming over here from Ireland to visit her soon, perhaps this spring. She was also thinking about renting out one of the rooms in the house. Although she wasn't strapped for money, it would bring in additional income for her. There were several rooms vacant upstairs and newly updated by her father. Mrs. Stedman made some coffee and she cut a piece of Erin's freshly baked apple pie. The snow was sticking to the windows and the streets were becoming covered. Several logs in the fireplace were burning. Stella told her she would have to make a decision. "Once you do, you have to stick with it.

Several weeks went by and she hadn't received a letter from Terrance. She decided not to write asking if everything was fine with him. Instead, she would wait and see what her uncle Peter had to say in his next letter. Erin and Albert continued to date, spending many hours at his country club. She would have to be signed in as an invited guest by Albert. There were trips to Boston where they would visit the museums or the port of Boston, where most of the fine dining was situated. She loved to shop in the many department stores that were open until late at night. Albert took her to only the elite establishments. And somehow, during the course of the evening, Albert would produce a flask containing some imported whiskey or scotch.

The entire state of Massachusetts was expanding with good times. Everyone was flourishing with money to spend. Nine months passed with only an occasional letter from Terrance. Erin believed she didn't press the matter enough and that was why Terrance was hesitant about visiting her. He most likely had a girlfriend and was probably thinking marriage. Albert had asked her several times to marry him. But Erin kept putting him off. She wasn't sure how she would be accepted by the Mandeville family. She wasn't even sure if she loved Albert. They hadn't made love yet, and that was another thing bothering Albert. It was constantly on his mind. He brought the subject up every time they were alone.

During the summer months, Dublin receives showers just about every day. Terrance entered Dawson's Pub at just a little after 8:00 p.m. The pub was established eighty years ago by Tyrone Dawson. Later his son Tyrone Dawson Jr. took it over, and it was now owed by a cousin named Frank Hagan. It was located in the middle of McConnell Street, in Dublin. It was packed with the usual patrons. Hagan was a heavy man with a bulging stomach in his late fifties and partially bald. He was a jolly sort but could turn to anger on a dime if annoyed by a drunken or a rowdy customer. The food was excellent and the bar had an assortment of beers and ales. The place was a moneymaker and the owner insisted on cash, with no trust.

Terrance asked the bartender for a dark ale. There was not a seat to be had, but it didn't bother Terrance to stand. This way, he could see who was in the place. He noticed a table full of girls sitting near the dartboard. The five of them all had beers. They were laughing and sometimes whispering to one another. All appeared to be the same age, probably in their early twenties or late teens. Bob Haskins came in and shouted out Terrance's name. During the last year, he had become friends with Haskins and they often associated together at the pubs. They enjoyed each other's company and made the rounds together whenever they went out chasing girls.

"Let's get a table," suggested Haskins.

They found one in the middle of the room, a couple of tables over from where the five girls were sitting.

"So what have you been up to?" asked Haskins.

"Working every day, same as you. Nothing really changes now, does it?" said Terrance.

"Terrance, you work much too hard for your own good. Get yourself a steady girl and let her take care of you. Let her work and you can relax and enjoy life," said Haskins. Terrance enjoyed Haskins's company, but he could be such a squirrel at times.

"You have everything going for you—looks, personality, and a good job. You can build just about anything," said Haskins.

"Not really," replied Terrance.

"You have something else you don't even know you have," said Haskins.

"And what is that?" inquired Terrance halfheartedly.

"It's a five letter word called charm. Why do you think most girls take one look at you and want you in bed?" replied Haskins.

Haskins continued telling Terrance that his charm was why women found him irresistible.

"It's the way you relate to them. Immediately, they want you. That is what charm will do for you, my friend."

Terrance kept glancing over at where the five girls were sitting. He couldn't help smiling after hearing his friend's words.

One of the girls wearing a yellow-and-green dress caught Terrance's eye. She looked at him and smiled. He knew the smile; he'd seen it before. He knew what she wanted and she was being coy. She and one of her girlfriends left the table and walked passed him toward the ladies room. She kept her eyes on him as she was walking, but when she came near to his table, she suddenly looked away. He was able to get a good look at her as she passed by. You could call her a little above average. Nice build, reddish brown hair in a ponytail. Terrance knew he had to talk to the girl to tell if she was his style. Terrance told Haskins to wait there as he left for the bar. When he reached the bar, the girl was waiting for him. She now had a bright smile on her face and took Terrance's arm.

"I'm Eliza," she said.

The girl wore a white sweater over her dress and up close looked to have creamy complexion. Her face was perfect, with no blemishes. Terrance introduced himself and offered the girl a beverage.

"Beer would be fine," she said.

There was music in the background, two fiddlers and a guitarist. All three sang an Irish ballad. Terrance looked over to where he had been sitting with Haskins, but Bob had left and was now on the dance floor with one of Eliza's girlfriends. Eliza took Terrance's hand and led him out to the dance floor. She wrapped her arm round his broad shoulders, looked up at him, and said, "I was waiting for you all night." Their cheeks touched. They never heard the music only their pounding hearts; both were thinking about later on in the evening when they would be alone.

The following morning, when Terrance awoke, his head was throbbing. He had too many shots of beers and Irish whiskey. He sat on the edge of the bed and placed both hands on his face. He was naked and still tired. He contemplated going back to sleep. Instead, he went into the bathroom to wash his face and hands. He still felt like a fish out of water. He opened the porch door and went out on the landing. It was overcast and cool. The street outside was empty except for a man having a coffee at a sidewalk café. He checked his watch. It was a little after 9:00 a.m.

The cool breeze felt good against his face. He returned to the room and saw the girl sleeping on her side. She was also naked. She was half covered by a white sheet. He thought of what she said to him when he first kissed her in bed. "I'm new to this." He asked her if this was her first time. She said something he couldn't understand, for he was as intoxicated as she. She mumbled other words that were inaudible to him. Words didn't mean anything now anyway. He stood looking at her thinking about how she performed last night. She was no virgin, this he knew. He knew most girls used this expression with guys just prior to lovemaking. It made them feel more in control. As he approached the bed, she now looked rather young. He considered waking her but changed his mind. It would serve no real purpose as she would probably want more sex, and right now, he was uninterested. He took a sponge bath, dressed, and decided it was time to leave. As he walked out of the hotel, he wondered how Haskins had made out, if he made a connection for the evening. That girl he was dancing with did look appealing. It was Sunday, a day of leisure for him.

Terrance took the train into Neary then the bus to Downey Lock. He wanted to talk to Peter and ask how Erin was making out since she had been left on her own. Terrance found him at Massey's Pub. Peter explained to him that she was well and was dating a well-to-do man who just recently completed his studies at the university. Peter wanted to make it clear to Terrance that Erin wasn't waiting around for him to rescue her. In fact, she was making out quite well without him. Peter asked him if he was staying in Dublin permanently. He told Peter he thought he might as well, given that he foresaw no real future in Downey Lock. Terrance thought to himself it would be best to remain silent about his plans to go to America. Peter told him the people in Downey Lock would miss him. Peter also revealed that Mae was expecting their third child due in September. Terrance smiled and wished him luck with the new addition to his family, ordering a couple more beers for them to celebrate.

Peter's boat was doing fine, but he thought of getting a larger one soon. The McGuire brothers came into the pub and ordered two beers with shots of Irish whiskey for chasers. Bart then walked over to Peter and asked him how everything was. They talked for a few moments before Bart left for the bar again. There was no longer a dispute between them. Bart and his brother had even attended Jack's memorial at Saint Michael's Church.

14

Jarvis and Freda Mandeville were now worried about their son Albert. They knew he was very fond of the young girl who lived in the big house by the ocean. He visited Erin every day and spent a considerable amount of time with her. They were embarrassed and didn't know how to prevent it. There were other problems too. Some of the government contracts were cancelled and work was slowing down. Wall Street was slowing as well. Stocks were changing and not for the better. Some of their friends were uneasy and talking about the difficult economy ahead.

August was a hot month, but it was enjoyable for Erin as the cool winds off the ocean provided a great deal of relief. She and Albert had plans to spend the evening in Boston listening to a concert. Never in her life did she believe she would indulge in such activities. She always lived such a simple life. Albert mentioned something regarding a baseball game. He told her of players running around with red stockings and hitting a ball with a large stick. He said they played this silly game in the Fenway section of Boston. Her life could no longer be considered dull. If Albert had one negative aspect, it was his occasional rudeness to ordinary people who didn't interpret his instructions correctly the first time. He disliked repeating himself. If he told a joke and you didn't get the main point, it irritated him to no end. He refused to repeat the joke or explain the ending to you. These were the times Erin considered Albert a snob and thought he may have inherited this trait from his parents. They could also be rude to people they felt lived beneath them.

The Mandevilles had scheduled a dinner party for the following Saturday evening with approximately forty guests attending. There would be the usual small-piece trio of background music to soften the atmosphere. The Mandevilles employed three servants for their household. The last girl they hired, Hannah Boarden, was a nineteen-year-old black girl of African descent from Chicago. She was a poor girl who ended up doing cleaning work in the churches of Boston. This was her first job as far as being a servant in a rich household, and she knew she was always being watched, as she was disciplined several times for unsatisfactory performance. She hated working for them but she needed the job and the money. Furthermore, she had her own room in the servant's quarters, which she thought was quite nice. In her room, she could be alone and think about her future plans. She really wanted to live back in Boston and learn a trade. She wanted to be self-sufficient, on her own, and not strapped down with the Mandevilles.

When Albert arrived, he met Erin in the courtyard and kissed her cheek. He told her how beautiful she looked. She told him how uneasy she was meeting everyone tonight and how she would love to avoid them.

"You will do fine, I'm sure," said Albert.

She wore a black dress with a white collar. It fitted her perfectly. She knew from the way they looked at her, without ever a smile or a look of acceptance, that his family didn't approve of her. Albert told her there would be several dignitaries from Boston and the Cape Cod area present.

Everyone was greeted on the front grounds of the Mandeville mansion where they were directed into the sunroom for cocktails. Some guests had on dinner jackets and ties while others wore suits and ties. After cocktails, the guests went to the dining room for dinner. On the tables were fruit and assorted cheeses imported from Europe. No liquor was displayed. Bottles of wine would be brought in later while the dinner was being served. People of wealth had no problem laying their hands on liquor whenever necessary. The majority was smuggled in from England to the ports of Boston. With the right connection, you could purchase what you needed.

Jarvis sat at the head of the table with his wife on his left. On his right sat Albert with Erin beside him. It was an exquisite meal. Roast duck, roast beef, assorted potatoes and vegetables. The desserts consisted of three different puddings. The talk at the table revolved around the slow economy, but no one appeared overly concerned. There was a discussion regarding the dues increasing at the country club, which elicited some laughter. "Every year they raised the dues and the green fees. There is no need of it," argued Clark McVerry. Jarvis told everyone they could join him in the sunroom for a cigar. Hannah Boarden, the servant girl, was instructed by Jarvis to open the locked cabinets in the sunroom and bring two bottles of brandy to one of the tables. She was then instructed to pour small amounts of brandy into the glasses that were also on the table. The guests would then help themselves to the brandy. No one in the room refused and all eventually picked up one of the glasses. One of the guests raised his brandy and presented a toast, "To the end of prohibition!" Everyone in the room roared with laughter. One of the guest asked Hannah if she would go and get him another brandy. When the girl gave the glass to the guest, he lost his grip and the glass fell to the floor. At the time, Jarvis was in the hallway and saw the mishap. Completely embarrassed by the incident, he hollered "complete stupidity on your part!" to Hannah.

"Please forgive me for this incompetent servant, sir. I have had problems with her in the past," related Jarvis.

The gentleman told Jarvis it was an accident on his part really.

"I should have held the glass tighter. I know the loss of good brandy is nothing to sneer at, but the girl did nothing wrong, Jarvis. It was my fault."

Jarvis dismissed the girl and told her to get on with her duties assisting the other guests.

Erin was in the hallway and saw the entire incident. The man was looking away when he was given the glass of brandy and it slipped out of his hand. She saw how annoyed Jarvis was, and the look on his face spelled doom for the servant girl. The party was a delight and it ended near midnight. Albert took Erin's hand and walked her outside for some fresh air. He kissed her and they left for her home. The following day she was told by a friend that Hannah had been dismissed because of the incident. Erin spoke to the girl on several occasions when she had been at the Mandeville's mansion with Albert. On one occasion when she was delivering goods to the Mandeville's house, she thought she saw someone in Hannah's room. She saw a glimpse of two individuals close together, almost touching. At the time, Erin thought nothing of it, believing it must have been a close friend. She found the girl to be bright and quite capable.

During the afternoon of the next day, Hannah Boarden came to see Erin at her house. Erin was doing gardening in the courtyard when Hannah asked her if she could speak to her. Erin welcomed the girl and led her to one of the nearby benches. Hannah explained how she had been dismissed from her work at the Mandevilles. They gave her a week's salary and refused to write any references for her.

"I have little money with no place to go."

She asked if it would be possible for her to stay at Erin's house, saying that the cellar or any other vacant room would be fine. She was leaving on the 10:00 a.m. train for Boston in the morning and promised she would not be a bother. She would be willing to pay whatever Erin asked.

It was then that Hannah broke down and began to cry. Holding one of her hands to her mouth, she continued to sob. Trying to comfort her, Erin placed her arm around the girl. She told her she had a room for her and encouraged her not to worry. She had planned to rent this room out in the near future anyway. It was vacant, and for one night, she didn't want her money. She took Hannah into the house and brought her into the kitchen to make some hot tea. Afterward, she showed her to a room near the kitchen, telling her she may stay there for the night. With the original owner, it was a servant's room. It was relatively small, but nice and warm in the winter since it was next to the kitchen.

"It is so nice of you to allow me to stay the night. You are a very kind woman," said Hannah.

They talked over tea and Hannah wondered aloud why she was so disliked by the Mandevilles.

"Did the other servants have any problems?" asked Erin.

"Not that I noticed, but I wasn't always with them. They never complained to me." Erin asked if it could be a racial matter. Hannah didn't believe it was.

"Why would they employ me in the first place?"

When Erin came downstairs to the kitchen the following morning, she was surprised to find Hannah was already up, the coffee was made, and the eggs and bacon were sizzling. Hannah said, "I am accustomed to getting up early and cooking breakfast for everyone including the other servants and the housekeeper. I have another two hours before my train leaves."

Erin was delighted with having breakfast served to her. The two continued to converse about how life can be so difficult for some people yet so easy for others. Erin could see that Hannah was sad as tears came to her eyes.

"I will do my best to make it on my own when I get to Boston. Of course, being black doesn't make it any easier," she said as she smiled at Erin.

Erin thought a moment and then asked Hannah if she wished to stay for another day or two.

"I have some work you can help me with if you like. I was thinking about hiring a girl."

Hannah's dark eyes brightened, and with a smiling face, she enthusiastically accepted the offer, exclaiming, "Yes, I would like that very much!"

Erin told her she was still thinking of renting out one of the other rooms upstairs. She was sure there wouldn't be a problem, but she wanted someone who could be trusted. The house was big enough, so maybe it could bring in some dividends.

Hannah Boarden never made it to the train station. Instead, she stayed on and assisted Erin in the house. For a room off the kitchen and food whenever she wanted it, she became an assistant to Erin. She knew her place and did what was asked of her by Erin. She was given an allowance every Thursday but saved the money because she had no living expenses.

Mrs. Agnes Seevin, a widow in her early sixties, was the first boarder to rent a room in the seaside house. She had lost her husband to cancer several years ago and was now living alone on the second floor in Snugport. Not long afterward, another guest rented a room at the Seaside Lodge. Weeks later, yet another came to live by the sea. They were drawn to the home's conditions. The place was spotless, the food excellent, and the view of the ocean unimaginable. Erin did all the cooking and baking, with help from Hannah, who became a pleasure to have around the lodge. The dining room was open to the public on Fridays, serving fish dinners and other foods. Her dinners were exciting and palatable and word spread fast regarding her Friday feasts. Erin decided to open up the dining room on the weekends. The dining room had eight tables and they were constantly filled. Some people thought her prices were high, but she told those that complained she used only the best ingredients to make her food so delicious.

Terrance sat back in his chair and peered out the window of the fast-moving train. It would be another two hours before he would arrive in Boston. The terrain was similar to the outskirts of Dublin with heavy bush and roaming hills. The rain pounding against the windows made it difficult to fully observe the landscape. Terrance first planned to get a room before seeing about the job he was offered. The company promised that with his experience they would have a place for him. He heard Boston was an Irish city, but not the most sociable. Terrance enjoyed looking out at the small towns and seeing some of the people working the fields. Heavy smoke coming from the chimneys signaled warmth inside the dwellings. He appreciated that because he knew how cold the cottages were in Downey Lock. He laid back his head thinking he would nap for a few minutes, but kept opening his eyes, fearing he would miss something. He could sleep, but didn't really want to.

Arriving at Boston's South Station, Terrance walked very little before finding the hotel of his choice. It was well past 3:00 p.m. so he thought he would rest in his room until morning. He had plenty of time to see the sights of Boston. What little he saw of New York was impressive. He enjoyed large cities and Dublin always amazed him. He noticed that the Boston streets and buildings were very similar to the ones in London. The old colony structures appeared mapped out in the same way as those in England. He felt quite at home. At the back of his mind, he hoped there wouldn't be a problem with his job and that the company hadn't changed their mind about hiring him.

The following morning, he met with some of the personnel people from the Rosetelli Builders Company. The company was in need of skilled carpenters and people who could read blueprints. Terrance would have no problems with either. He was to report to work on a new building under construction. He visited a café on Washington Street and sat down to a cup of coffee. From his coat pocket, he removed Erin's Snugport address. There was a train to the small village leaving at 12:05 p.m. and Terrance had every intention of taking it. He wondered what kind of greeting he would receive from Erin. It had been so long for them, so many years apart. What would they have in common, perhaps nothing? Terrance stared at the windowpane and followed the drops of rain as they rolled down the glass and vanished into the cracks on the bottom. Terrance stepped off the train, made a few inquiries, and was told he was but walking distance from Erin's house. As he walked along the road, he took in the ocean view and the stillness of the waves. They just seemed to float into the shore without any heavy movement. In the distance, he could see a lighthouse, which was blue on top and white on the bottom. He wondered if the lighthouse was in working condition, with the shoreline being as rocky as it was. Back in Downey Lock, the breakers would pound the shoreline like they were punishing it with some awful curse.

It was still raining slightly, but it appeared the sky was brightening up in the south. She wasn't expecting him and he hoped it wouldn't be too much of a shock. Terrance walked to the rear of the house and saw a black girl hanging sheets on a clothesline. He approached her and asked if Erin Browne was home. She looked him over from head to toe and said she was but he was to wait there while she went to notify her. The rain had stopped and there was a cool ocean breeze stroking the back of his neck. He heard footsteps coming from inside the house. The door opened and standing there was a young lady. She stared at the man in front of her, not recognizing who he was. He wore no hat and his raven black hair was parted on the left side reaching down to the nape of his neck. He wore a black jacket that went to his waist. His gray trousers were a tiny bit short allowing his white socks to show. His jacket was open in the front, revealing a red-and-green plaid shirt. He was clean shaven and he wore a bright smile.

"Hello, are you Erin? I am Terrance," he said.

Erin stood still, not moving a muscle. Yes, she replied not knowing what else to say. She found him to be a handsome young man, but even more, she was impressed with the way he presented himself. "Oh God, Terrance!" She ran into his arms and they both hugged for a minute and said nothing.

There were several park benches in the rear yard, and holding his hand, she led him to one. With their hands still clasped tightly, they just sat and looked at one another.

Finally, Erin broke the silence and spoke, "I am thrilled you are here, but why didn't you let me know you were coming?"

"So is this your new Downey Lock?" he said.

Both spoke with their Irish brogue, but his was more predominant.

"You are still lovely, Erin. Outside of being taller, you have changed very little." They both kept smiling and again began hugging each other. The two began talking at once and then laughed aloud. He immediately told her of his job in Boston as an assistant to one of the foreman in the carpenter's division. They were constructing a new building on Washington Street. She could see how enthusiastic he was, but couldn't tell if it was over his new employment or seeing her for the first time in nine years. He was such a joy to be around as he continued telling her of his exploits and what he wanted to accomplish in the future. She took his arm as he continued talking and they walked into the house. She told him she had to make dinner, but insisted he keep on talking about what he had planned. She wanted to hear everything about occurrences in Downey Lock. He told her of his placement in the home and of his good friend Brother John.

"Of course you will stay for dinner," she said.

"I don't want to put you out, Erin," he replied.

"Please I want to hear so much more."

She told him everything regarding her father and what had happened to her during the time she had been in America. She was at a long table in the kitchen. As she talked, she cut up some sort of meat that looked like chops. He didn't want to interrupt, but Erin had no problem talking and preparing food at the same time. Hannah was also in the kitchen, washing some vegetables and placing them in large containers to be cooked. She never said a word the entire time Erin and he conversed. She knew both of them needed this time together without interruption. While she had no idea who this young man was, she could tell he was important to Erin. She couldn't help overhearing them, and every now and then, she would smile while listening to their conversation. Erin listened intently as Terrance continued talking about Downey Lock. How Peter and Mae were doing fine and were in good health. How nothing had changed there. He told her he had to work in the morning and hoped to make a good impression. They both laughed. She assured him he would do fine and soon would be a major contributor to the construction company.

"We have dinner every evening at six p.m.," she said.

He asked if she did all the cooking. She told him she did with some help from Hannah. She went to cooking school and taught herself a few new recipes. He asked her if there was anyone special in her life right now. She told him about Albert and about how wealthy he was and how she wasn't sure where the courtship was going. He asked her if she was in love with him. Jolted by the question, she said she wasn't sure. Terrance liked that answer. If she was in love, wouldn't she know it? She went on saying she had taken in three boarders but still had two empty rooms she hoped to soon fill. She didn't mention anything about the money she inherited from her father or that the house had been paid off after his death.

The guests came down from their rooms and went to the day room, a room built for relaxation, with several large overstuffed chairs. The daily paper was always present on one of the tables nearby or on the floor beside a chair. There was always a bowl full of fresh popcorn for the guests to nibble on. Erin brought Terrance into the dayroom and introduced him to the lodgers. She left him there and returned to the kitchen. On the wall was a large picture of her father with the ocean in the background. The day room had a large picture window with a beautiful view of the ocean. Terrance couldn't keep his eyes off it.

"Isn't it a gorgeous sight," Mildred Benten, one of the lodgers, mused.

"Quite beautiful," said Terrance.

"Really, it's one of the reasons I came here, and of course, the food helps too." Terrance smiled at the elderly lady.

Mrs. Benten was in her late seventies and was a widow.

"I lost my husband twelve years ago. I was living in Florida, but I wanted to be near home again, near Boston."

Erin came back to the room, took Terrance's arm, and led him into the kitchen. On the table was a pie covered with blueberries. With a spoon, she removed some of the fruit and juices and told him to open his mouth then she placed the spoon inside. He smiled and raved at how delicious the pie was, even asking for a small piece before dinner. She told him he would have to wait. The three guests sat at separate tables. The dining room was cheerfully decorated with Old English wallpaper. Hanging from the ceiling was a large chandelier with multiple light bulbs. Cloth napkins were neatly displayed on every table wrapped with a knife, fork, and spoon. It was an elegant display.

15

Erin served dinner and Terrance stood by to watch the proceedings. He was impressed with the way Erin went about her work, making sure her guests were comfortable while Hannah stayed close by just in case any of the clientele wanted anything. When all the guests were served, Erin and Terrance took a table near a window.

"I can't believe you are such a responsible person," Terrance told Erin as he laughed.

"I had to grow up real fast," she explained.

"Your house is grand and I love the view of the sea."

"Thanks, Terrance."

She noticed Terrance looked tired, but he still had that spunk in him, which made him appear he could go on forever. She was curious to know what his feelings were for her. What she had to find out was what she thought of him. He had grown so much over the years, not only in body structure but in maturity. She was about to ask him if he wanted to stay overnight, but then remembered he had to work early in the morning. He never mentioned his father or mother and she thought that was strange. He only wanted to talk about Erin and how she accomplished what she had in such a short time, but she wanted to ask what his intentions were and if he was planning to return to Ireland. In the end, she thought it was too early to ask such questions. She could see by the expression on his face he enjoyed his dinner. The pork chops were fried with onions and a dash of pork sauce, her own recipe. He devoured the blueberry pie and had a second slice. Afterward, they went out to the rear porch that surrounded the dwelling to sit and chat some more.

He mentioned he had to catch the ten o'clock train back to Boston and it was thus time to leave. He told her he would come back soon. She informed him she was going to have a telephone connected in a few days and would give him the number. He thanked her for dinner and kissed her on the cheek. He walked away toward the village, stopped after approximately twenty yards, and waved to her. Smiling, she waved back. She noticed he didn't have any holes in his socks.

Hannah was cleaning up in the kitchen. Erin helped her but neither girl said a word. Hannah could see that her friend was blissful and was wondering where this mysterious man had come from and what he possessed that had such an influence on Erin.

It occurred so fast nearly everyone went into shock. The entire nation didn't know what to do. The stock market went crashing down into the pits of hell. And it took loads of people with it. People who were wealthy found themselves penniless. Even the middle class who had little savings lost whatever money they saved. The twenties had been good times for numerous citizens. Automobiles had taken over the new roads and radio had produced a new kind of entertainment. News from Europe could now be heard in your living room. It was an exciting time, but with the collapse of Wall Street, the future looked dim. Within weeks, the economy started slipping and jobs were lost. Huge corporations went under and bankruptcy was prevalent, occurring daily. The government had no answers and asked the people to stay calm. In New England, the textile business was stricken the hardest. Orders and contracts were no longer distributed, so buildings closed.

The Mandevilles' business was among those tumbling down. Jarvis Mandeville informed his wife that if the economy didn't improve soon they would have to close the factory. When the banks started closing, people were scared for their future. The media spoke of no rapid turnaround for the country. Europe was also experiencing troubled times. The voluminous Wall Street crash had now affected countries around the world. The bank in Snugport was still operating, but people wondered for how long. Erin was worried about her money in the bank. Everyone in the town spoke of the national disaster.

She kept thinking of Terrance and wondered why he had not come to see her. She had her telephone hooked up and wanted to give him her new number. She didn't even know his address in Boston. She thought it strange that he never came back or got in touch with her. It had been nine days now. Perhaps he had lost interest in her. That certainly could be a possibility. Maybe he is working so hard it is difficult for him to get away. She remembered telling him she was getting a telephone soon. Why did he not inquire about her number with the phone service?

Later that evening, she had a date with Albert. They were going to see a movie in Boston. She noticed Albert had been edgy lately, complaining about the family business. He recently purchased a new automobile and mentioned several times that he hoped he would be able to keep it despite the economic downturn. Erin didn't tell him about Terrance's appearance. He told her she shouldn't have taken in Hannah, that she would soon be trouble.

"My parents found her not to be trustworthy and lazy at times."

Erin just smiled and told him, "She knows she has to work here. She will be fine or she will leave. Anyway, don't worry about it. I want her here to assist me."

He was becoming more insistent about sex. He wanted to know who she was saving herself for.

Terrance was doing fine with his work. He enjoyed the people he was working with, but after the Wall Street crash, some of them were being laid off. Bernie Rufferson was Terrance's supervisor. Rufferson was on the job every day with Terrance, inspecting sites and going over the day's work. This was a government-funded construction project and was designed to be a building for workers in the government system. Several more projects like it were soon to be built in and around the Boston area. The Rosetelli Builders had the inside track for at least another site. While Terrance was explaining some work problems to one of the foreman, Rufferson came up to them and stood by until Terrance finished speaking. He told Terrance there was a meeting at 3:00 p.m. later that afternoon at their headquarters and he was expected to attend.

The construction firm had an office with several private rooms for meetings located in downtown Boston. Terrance acknowledged the order from his boss and was about to walk away when Rufferson placed his hand on his shoulder and assured him not to worry as it did not directly regard him.

"They want to speak to us about the third-floor landing and why it is taking so long to finish. It's just one of those regular meetings, Terrance."

"Why? Did I look worried?" asked Terrance.

"To me, you always look concerned about something," joked Rufferson.

What was really concerning Terrance was the fact that he constantly had Erin on his mind. Both at night and during work hours, he thought about her incessantly. One minute he wasn't sure if she was really happy to see him, and then, after thinking it over, he would change his mind and think differently. He was puzzled about her. He wondered why he felt this way about her. The last time he saw her, she was only ten year old. He'd been with other women but never had the feelings for them like he did for Erin. He tried to rationalize and thought to himself that it couldn't be love for love had to be nurtured. He had never held her in his arms or kissed her yet. What did he know about anything? The few times they were together in Ireland, it was just child play—the picnics, exploring caves, or chasing her through the fields. He planned on returning Saturday. It had been over a week since he had seen her last.

Terrance and Rufferson were still in their work clothes when they reported for the afternoon meeting. The owners of the company were there with several other supervisors, most of them in suits and ties. After more than an hour and thirty minutes, everyone had enough and wanted it to end. It was getting close to quitting time and they believed they had addressed many of the problems. During the meeting, Terrance noticed a blond girl standing in the neighboring room. The door was open so everyone in the room had no difficulty seeing her. She was extremely attractive—tall and thin with blue eyes. Her hair was golden, like the rays of the sun reflecting off a body of water. She had on a yellow skirt with a white blouse and was elegantly dressed. She was standing by a table with a few magazines, flipping through one of them and paying attention to no one in particular. She looked up and saw Terrance talking to several gentlemen. The men were all wearing suits and ties, except for two others who were wearing work clothes. The meeting was over and they all started walking toward her. One of the owners stopped and introduced his daughter to Terrance and Rufferson. "Say hello to my daughter Carolyn," spoke Louis Rosetelli.

They both acknowledged the striking and good-looking young lady. She shook both of their hands and smiled politely. She appeared a little shy but couldn't keep her eyes off Terrance. Terrance was taken in by her beauty and her presence. She asked Terrance if he was employed with her father's company. When he told her he was, she immediately wanted to know in what capacity. He told her he was assisting Mr. Rufferson, the head engineer. As they approached the elevators, the girl kept a steady eye on Terrance, who could feel the tension and never looked directly at the girl.

Carolyn could tell he was an immigrant by the way he spoke but she wasn't sure from what country. She was impressed by the way he handled himself among her father and the other high-ranking people of the company. She told them both she enjoyed meeting them. Terrance turned and looked at the girl, smiled, and nodded slightly. When the elevator arrived, it was almost full so Terrance and Rufferson let the others go and they stayed back to await the next one. The following morning, Terrance was working on one of the scaffolds that hung three stories up on the new office building. He was giving instructions to a worker about how to do a certain job on a balcony, which had to be connected to the building. He noticed a figure inside the room.

Standing alone was Carolyn Rosetelli. She said hello and he replied he was surprise to see her. She told him it took almost ten minutes to get here because the elevator was slow. She asked if she was disturbing him from his work. He said no and climbed into the room through the window. Terrance didn't know what to expect but saw the blond lady was still resplendent, now wearing a black skirt and a yellow blouse open just a little at the top. She said she liked coming up on the newly constructed building and watching the men work. She especially liked watching the finishing work. "It is watching people create something new, watching them bring it to life."

Terrance learned she was twenty-two years of age and had completed her education at Enson Wilson College here in Boston. Terrance found her pleasant to talk to and could see she was well-bred. She told him she was going to lunch soon and asked if he would like to join her. He told her he would enjoy having lunch with her and planned to meet her in front of the building at noontime. It was five minutes after noontime when he came down from the unfinished office building and she was waiting for him. They had lunch not far from where Terrance was working. It was a small place with only five tables, and two were taken. Terrance suggested the restaurant since he had eaten there in the past and enjoyed the food. Charlie's was one of the oldest eateries in Boston; some people said it was there during the revolution. She asked about his younger years while in Ireland, but since he found it troublesome, he avoided the topic of his childhood saying only that it was like that of any other boy growing up in Ireland. Terrance told her of the beautiful country that is Ireland. She said she had never been outside of Boston but saw pictures of the lush and green country and she was placing it on her list of places to visit.

She told him, "I love your Irish accent. I hope you never lose it, it is so charming." Terrance smiled and laughed softly. Her eyes were sparkling as if telling him a story. She couldn't get enough of him. And he now knew it. They were sitting together eating cold cut sandwiches and sipping soft drinks. Every now and then, they laughed together over some silly remark one of them made. Twice, she touched his hand while laughing. There was no doubt he was excited by her touch. He wondered where this was going. What did she want from him? She certainly had boyfriends, perhaps many.

"So are you seeing someone serious?" asked Terrance.

"If you mean, am I in love? No."

Terrance replied, "I wasn't sure, just thought I would ask."

"To be honest, I date often and most of the fellows are a few years older than me. I like it that way because I feel more secure. Kind of dumb, isn't it?"

"Of course not, many women have those kinds of feelings," said Terrance.

Changing the subject, he told her the building was going well, but hoped there wouldn't be a problem with completing it because of the economy. Everyone knew business was hurting throughout the country.

After they completed their lunch and as they stood to leave, she grabbed his arm and smiled at him, saying, "We are having a dinner party at my house Friday night. It would be nice if you could come. I mean I don't want you to break your plans if you have any."

"I have no plans and I would love to attend. Thank you for inviting me, Carolyn. Where exactly do you live?"

"Why don't I pick you up at your place?" she suggested. "You don't have an automobile, do you?"

"No. I am using the buses, but I get around well enough," he said with a smile.

She told him lunch was on her since she suggested they meet.

"Please allow me," Terrance urged.

But she insisted and paid the waiter.

The rest of the day, Terrance had a difficult time concentrating on his work. He kept thinking about the young beauty and wondered what to expect from her at the dinner party. He knew he would eat well, but he wondered how her parents would receive him. She was a classy lady, and he was sure her parents would have something to say about the Irishman coming to dinner.

After work, Terrance went to a phone booth to call information and obtain Erin's phone number. They discussed him coming over for Saturday night and perhaps catching a movie in town. He said he would be over sometime after five o'clock. Erin was now inspired to make a delicious dinner for him. After dinner was over, she and Hannah sat at the kitchen table, needing a rest after serving dinner to the guests.

"Would you like me to make some fresh tea for us?" asked Hannah.

Erin said nothing and looked out the window at the light snow falling to the ground. "My mother always told me that the first dropping of snow never sticks to the ground. I have no idea where she got that from. It might have been an old Irish tale."

This November was colder than usual and the snow was a surprise to most in Snugport. Erin was in a good mood. She instructed Hannah to go downstairs to the cellar. Next to the coal pit was a door that led into another section of the cellar. On a shelf, she would find a coffee can with a key in it. She was to unlock the door across from the shelf and bring up a bottle of French champagne.

When Hannah open the door, she discovered the room was filled with all sorts of alcohol including whiskeys from all across Europe, the best Scotch whiskey from Scotland, and some of the finest wines from Italy and France. They were all still in their original cases. Hannah was astonished to see all that alcohol, wondering where in the world it came from. The room had a damp smell as though no one had entered it in ages. Yet there was a distinct aroma of alcohol in the air. She retrieved the bottle of French champagne from one of the cartons. There was a table in the room and Hannah noticed it had a drawer in it. With her curiosity heightened, she pulled out the drawer and inside discovered wadded rolls of money. There were hundreds of dollars wrapped in elastic bands. She picked up the bands of money in both hands only to let them fall back into the drawer. There had to be thousands of dollars. She had to steady herself as she closed the drawer. She felt a little faint. In her entire life, she never saw so much money in one place or at one time. She wondered if Erin even knew the money was there since her father died so suddenly. There was the possibility that just maybe she didn't. Hannah opened the drawer again and stared at all the money.

Erin must know the money is in this drawer in this locked room, she thought.

She tried to replace the money in the same order it was when she first opened the drawer and then closed it. She reminded herself that this was not her money.

She came upstairs with the bottle of champagne and sat it on the table.

Erin said, "I never really thought sparkling wine was that tasteful. Please, Hannah, would you open the bottle as I have never been able to in the past."

Hannah smile and said, "Oh, I have opened many bottles. It's simple."

She took the bottle of champagne in her left hand and removed the wiring around the cap and then with her right thumb pried the cork upward. The champagne came rushing out, and the cork, traveling at such a fast pace, struck the ceiling and came back and smacked Erin on the head. They both laughed and ran for some towels to clean up the mess.

"Please get two of our best glasses from the cupboard," said Erin.

Hannah poured the champagne in the two glasses and then inquired into the reason for such celebration.

Erin told her friend, "The fellow you met last week is returning Saturday evening for dinner."

Hannah told Erin, "I can't believe what I saw down there, all that wonderful booze. Really, where did you get all of it?"

Erin explained to Hannah her father had come into possession of it as a truck driver. "You mean to tell me your daddy was a rum runner!" she burst out, laughing.

They drank almost the entire bottle and were now talking loudly and boisterously. They found everything they said amusing and they continued roaring with laughter over silly comments that were far from humorous. Hannah enjoyed the time, especially since she had rarely seen Erin truly happy. Erin herself couldn't remember the last occasion that was so pleasurable. She liked Hannah and thought her to be not only trustworthy, but entertaining. Nothing seemed to bother her. As her father used to say, some people just float with the tide.

The clock in the downstairs hallway read 3:00 a.m. A figure in dark clothing, holding a lighted candle in its hand opened the cellar door and proceeded down the wooden stairs. Even with the candle illuminating the cellar, there was very little light. Still, this individual had little problem finding the way around in the darkened room. The coffee can was found and the key it contained was removed. The key was inserted into the lock and the door opened. The person proceeded directly to the drawer, placed the candle above it, and looked inside. The money was disturbed; it was not in its correct place. With the illumination from the candle, the dark figure counted the bands of money. The money was all there. No bands were missing. Erin didn't think her friend would steal from her and felt guilty for having her doubts, but at least now she was satisfied and could completely trust Hannah in the future.

The Mandevilles were suffering badly. Their business was slow and in real danger of closing. Bills were piling up significantly and all of their servants were let go. Jarvis wondered what the future held for him, his wife, and his younger son. Talking over the family situation, he and his wife thought it might be best if Albert married the girl he wanted as his wife. During breakfast, Jarvis informed Albert that he wanted him to understand that he and his mother had no intentions of interfering in his life.

"You can marry whoever you want. If it is the young girl with the house by the ocean, so be it."

This had Albert wondering about the sudden change in their attitude. He knew his parents didn't think Erin was the best choice for him.

"If I am capable of taking over the family business, I know who I want by my side when I have to make important decisions," said Albert.

He told both his father and mother he was in love with Erin and wanted her as his wife. On more than one occasion, Albert had hinted that he wanted to marry Erin, but she was always hesitant.

"The problem is, I am not really sure she loves me," sulked Albert.

While Carolyn was driving Terrance to her house, he was taken aback by some of the beautiful homes on Beacon Hill. The neighborhood was marked by gas-lit streets and brick sidewalks. The rows of houses were so elegantly designed that some people in Boston called them millionaire's row.

Certainly, Terrance had never seen anything like it before. He was in complete awe of the entire neighborhood and felt uneasy as they drove into the large driveway of the dwelling. Carolyn took his hand and smiled as they walked to the front door where they were met by her mother. Claire Rosetelli cordially invited Terrance into her home while a servant removed his black leather coat. He was wearing a white shirt with blue trousers and polished black shoes. He was cleanly shaven. Carolyn was outfitted in a black dress that fell a few inches below her knees. To most of the younger crowd, she was striking. Terrance was offered cocktails and then asked by Carolyn to leave the family room and go with the rest to the library. He told her he was fine with just a simple soft drink. She kept hold of his hand to make sure he didn't escape somewhere.

While dining, the conversation was about the economy and what the future held. At times, it drifted to sports. The Red Sox had played through another awful season. Everyone agreed Boston was exciting and growing extremely fast. Carolyn sat next to Terrance at the center of the table where once or twice she would take hold of Terrance's hand under the table and squeeze it. While waiting for dessert, she placed her fingers on his thigh and he felt an electric shock penetrate through his body. He almost shouted out in alarm, he was so surprised. She just stared at him, saying nothing, and he wondered if anyone else at the table knew what was happening. He looked down and sipped his soda, looking up again at Carolyn only to find that she continued staring at him. This was quickly becoming a very embarrassing situation.

Claire Rosetelli asked him if he enjoyed working in Boston. Terrance was able to shift his legs far away enough from Carolyn's hand to respond that he found Boston to be a great city and felt quite fortunate to be working there. The evening went by quickly for Terrance and he thought Carolyn's entire family was extremely pleasant. At the end of the evening, the two drove to his apartment, where Terrance experienced a little difficulty getting away from Carolyn. She was in no hurry to leave his apartment even though he told her ladies were prohibited there after ten o'clock.

She smiled and responded with "okay, I get the point." After the last kiss, she told him, "I think you're wonderful. Please call me soon."

He smiled, touched her cheek with his fingers, and watched her leave. He truly thought she was lovely but couldn't shake the feeling that there was trouble ahead. He wondered where this affair was going.

Terrance said nothing to Erin about Carolyn and what was going on between them. Saturday evening was very enjoyable for him. Again they talked about nothing except their times together in Downey Lock. She was concerned about what was happening with her uncle Peter and his family. Erin told Terrance during dinner that she wanted to take him to meet the family who took her in when she so desperately needed help. The Stedmans were overjoyed at meeting Erin's friend from Ireland, deeming him quite handsome and most polite. Terrance had a way of making a first impression such that when people met him, they immediately liked him. There was no wait to see if his personality changed or if he would disappoint you in another fashion. Maybe that was the charm he possessed. He was an enthusiastic listener and always kept eye contact with whoever he was speaking with. Along with his other qualities, this impressed the Stedmans. Erin asked the Stedmans how they were coping with the economy. She wanted to be sure that everything was fine with them. Mr. Stedman said they were doing as well as anyone else in town, but Erin looked at Stella and sensed there was something wrong. Stella then mentioned that they were considering closing their retail store.

"We aren't doing the business we were doing in the past. People just don't have the money and we can't continue giving out credit to so many poor individuals. They promise to pay, but with no money coming in, they are unable to."

For the first time in many months, Erin felt sad. She felt she should have paid more attention to what was happening to her foster parents. These were decent people and she loved them dearly.

Erin said, "Please tell me how much money you need and I will write a check for you immediately. You know I have the money and it is yours anytime you ask. I have never forgotten your kindness in the past."

The Stedmans wanted nothing from Erin but her love. Erin refused to negotiate the matter any longer and told them she wanted to help them. That was final. The entire time, Terrance sat without speaking a word. He took in everything that was discussed but didn't intrude on the discussion. He marveled at the way Erin spoke to the Stedmans. He could see her love for them just by the way she expressed herself. The following day she sent out a substantial check to the Stedmans. Included in the envelope was a note expressing her love.

16

The next day, Sunday, Albert Mandeville came to Erin's for breakfast. She was pleased to see him in an ebullient mood. She noticed a large difference between him and Terrance. Albert was so open and up-front about everything. He couldn't wait to tell you of the town gossip or any other news he stumbled upon. Yet she sensed he was insecure when making decisions on his own. He started with small talk, asking how her business was responding during these dark days, if she was financially secure, and if she had lost any money in the bank. She assured him she was holding up fine. Finally, he revealed to her that he was worried the family business may go under, as his father was having difficulty receiving loans from the banks.

It was one of those dreary days when the sun was lost in the shadows of the dark sky. Albert caught a glimpse of some rain dropping down on the outside veranda and told Erin he had a feeling this was going to be a miserable day.

"I love the rain," she replied with a happy tone.

Albert said, "I don't understand why you keep that girl around here, knowing my family fired her."

Erin replied, "Hannah is my friend. She is a big help to me here."

Albert turned the conversation back to the two of them, mentioning how long they had been together. He bluntly asked her what her feelings were for him.

"Do we have to go through this again? Please, Albert, not this morning. You know I think you're a fine man and a real fun person. Why must we make this complicated?"

"Do you love me?" asked Albert.

"I am not sure," stammered Erin.

Albert wanted to know if marriage was in her plans. He told her he wanted her to be his wife and bear his children. She looked away without answering. Albert became angry.

"What the hell is the matter with you? Is there a problem?" he scowled.

She still didn't say anything. She was annoyed by his questioning. He could see she was becoming upset and he thought it best not to force her. Erin wasn't quite sure how to handle Albert any longer. He was certainly good to her, and he had bought her many presents since they had been seeing each other, even mentioning he wanted to buy her a new automobile. She refused, saying she didn't want nor need a new car because her vehicle was running good enough. A month ago, he wanted to go hunting up in Maine close to the Canadian border. He had wanted her to go with him, but she refused, saying she couldn't leave her business or the lodge. The resentment he had for Hannah bothered her too. Why didn't he like Hannah staying here at the lodge with her? He also didn't like the idea of her letting out rooms to individuals. Why would that upset him? She had two more rooms for rent but didn't intend to advertise them in the local papers because she knew someone would be interested in the near future.

Several days later, Erin received a phone call from Dorothy Sinclare of the local library, asking if she could come over at Erin's convenience. What could this woman want from her after being so difficult after her father's death? That afternoon, at approximately 2:00 p.m., they had tea at the lodge. Ms. Sinclare wanted to know if she had a room available for her at the lodge. She heard nothing but rave reviews about the lodge, from its cleanliness to its reasonable rates.

"I know we have not been the best of friends and I will understand if you refuse me," said Ms. Sinclare.

She informed Erin that where she was living now was a problem as the landlord wanted her apartment for someone else.

"I believe it is for one of his relatives," she said.

Erin replied, "I do have a room available, and yes, you may have it if you want it."

She showed the room to her new prospective guest. Sinclare was delighted with the room and agreed to move in sometime next week. She paid Erin two weeks in advance. They finished their tea, and upon leaving, the librarian expressed her hope that the two of them would become good friends. Erin could see a different kind of personality in the librarian since she had last seen her, but then again, was there a secret agenda for wanting a room at the lodge? Erin would just have to wait and see.

Sunday was cold and snow was forecasted. Erin told Hannah she would be gone for most of the day, traveling to Boston with Stella to do some shopping. After lunch with her foster parents, Erin was asked by Stella if they could postpone their trip to Boston as she had a headache.

"We could make it any other day you like, Erin, but today I don't feel well. Just tell me when and I will be ready to go."

Erin didn't really care and said they could go whenever she was in better spirits. It was 1:20 p.m. when she kissed them both and left for home.

She drove around to park at the rear of the lodge and entered through the back door of the kitchen as she wanted to speak to Hannah regarding dinner. Hannah wasn't in the kitchen. She wasn't in the dining room either. The door to Hannah's room was closed. She was about to knock on the door when she heard voices. She waited. At first, the voices were muffled, but then she could make out Hannah's voice speaking in a soft tone. For a moment, she thought she heard a man's voice.

"No, it couldn't be," said Erin.

She thought for a moment if she should open the door. She was hesitant to open it and thought it would be terrible if what she was thinking was wrong. Her hand had already turned the doorknob and suddenly the door was wide open. She saw what she expected when she looked into the room.

There was a gasp and then Erin saw them both. Hannah was in her bed, and next to her was Albert, both without a stitch of clothes on. Their clothing was hung on a chair on the other side of the room. Neither of them said anything. All three were too ashamed to make any kind of remark at all. Finally, Erin spoke with her eyes on fire and demanded both of them to leave her house. Hannah lay back in bed and drew the sheet up to her neck and looked away. Albert got out of bed still naked and walked to the chair where his clothes were and put them on. "I want you out of the house within the hour," Erin told Hannah as she approached the bed. Then she glanced over at Albert who was still straightening out his clothes and told him she wanted him out of her life forever. Erin then remembered the time she saw someone at the window of Hannah's room when she was employed by the Mandevilles. It appeared to be a male figure close to Hannah, and now Erin understood that the figure had been Albert.

Erin realized that he had been seeing her every chance he had in order to release his sexual tensions. There is no telling how many times he had been with her. What a fool she was to think he was someone special. While leaving, Albert made an effort to do some explaining, but Erin would hear none of it.

Then he said, "This would not have happened if you weren't so damn cold all the time. I wouldn't have to go elsewhere for sex!"

"It's over! Get out!" screamed Erin.

As Albert was about to leave through the kitchen door, Hannah entered and asked if he would give her a ride. He turned to her, said nothing, went to his car, and drove away. Hannah looked at Erin and wanted to say something, but thought the better of it and left with her bags.

Erin made some tea for herself and sat down at the kitchen table to think over the situation. How could I believe marriage was possible with that man? She also wondered what feelings Hannah had for Albert. Was she in love with him? There was no telling how many times they had been together and it could be possible that Hannah was indeed in love with him. She was glad to have both of them out of her life. Erin thought of Hannah's firing and wondered if the Mandevilles somehow discovered their son was having sex with the girl. What a scandalous affair that would produce were it ever to be made public.

A few days later, while she was outside hanging a wash, she heard the doorbell ring. She knew instantly it was coming from the front door so she hurried to get there. A man in his late thirties stood at the doorway. He was of rugged build and average height. He was clean shaven outside of sporting a neatly trimmed mustache. He told Erin he was inquiring about a room he heard might be available. She invited him in and brought him to the dining room where he introduced himself as Carl Hosten. He was a teacher in the Boston school system and left on his own accord. He was now working on a novel. At forty years of age and in excellent health, Hosten seemed to be an intellectual-type person with good manners. Erin asked if he had any references.

"Of course," he replied. "Just tell me when you want them and I will get them."

He asked if meals came with the room and was told they did. Erin asked again about the references but the statement appeared to go over his head as he gazed out the window, taking in the view of the sea. He spoke that he loved the ocean and wanted someday to sail away to some Caribbean island and continue his writing. She asked if he was presently employed. He said he wasn't but he had enough finances for the foreseeable future. He continued by saying that with his education finding work wouldn't be a problem.

"When my book is published soon, I will have all the capital I will ever need."

He got up from his seat and went to the window for a closer look at the sea. He turned to Erin and told her she had a beautiful piece of property.

Then he asked, "Will you accept me here at your lodge?"

She decided he could have the room but asked for a month's advance. Erin wasn't yet sure if she was going to get another helper to assist her at the lodge or do it alone. She thought it might be better if she had someone come in and take care of the rooms for the guests. She would like a young girl that could assist her with the cooking too. With the economy being so poor, there would surely be many young girls looking for such an opportunity.

Terrance received a phone call from Carolyn inviting him to a concert at Symphony Hall in Boston on Friday evening. Fast tunes were now the popular genre. Along with swinging jazz music, the Charleston was everyone's new favorite. Terrance didn't care much for classical music, but he told her he would accompany her and would be waiting downstairs on the street. The music was loud and wonderful. Terrance was surprised by how much he enjoyed it. A couple of rows to the right of him and Carolyn sat her parents. Every now and then, Carolyn's mother would glance over at them to see if they were enjoying the music. As soon as the concert was over, Carolyn took Terrance's hand and whispered to him.

"Let's get out of here quickly before we are stopped by the most boring people and are asked to explain the entire concert to them."

Not far from the concert hall, they stopped into one of the jazz clubs to hear some other kind of music. There were three black musicians whacking out their instruments— sax, trombone, and drums. The place was packed with jazz enthusiasts. Every table had alcohol on it. For sure, no one in the club would have passed a sobriety test. Prohibition at this moment meant nothing. Not only in Boston, but in all of the large cities in the country, the authorities weren't even bothering to enforce the laws pertaining to alcohol.

Terrance and Carolyn were able to get a table not far from the dance floor. Within minutes, they were on the dance floor doing the Charleston. Terrance never danced to the Charleston before but he found it rather easy. There was no way to deny it; this was a fun night for him. Judging by the expression on Carolyn's face, she wasn't unhappy either. Over drinks, Carolyn asked if everything was going well between them. Terrance smiled and told her of course. He wondered why she asked such a question and thought she may be insecure. They only had a few dates and wondered what she was after. Was it marriage? Terrance was in no hurry for a blasting romance. He liked this young blond girl and that was it. He didn't know what love was like because he had never been in love before.

He was sure he wasn't in love with Carolyn. Terrance believed as pretty as Carolyn was and even with her amiable personality, she lacked a sense of humor. She was a very serious person and at times forced her smiles. She disliked being in the presence of difficult people and individuals who loved to talked about themselves.

She told him, "I have no idea where you are going, I just hope you will let me come with you."

He was intrigued by what she said but told her ever since he was a boy he traveled alone.

"I have a good job now but I don't know what the future entails."

The music was so loud they had a difficult time hearing each other. Terrance sipped his gin and tonic and wondered if it was bathroom gin. He doubted if anyone could tell the difference. Carolyn's coat was hung over the back of her chair. It was brown fur and it came to her waist. He kept his eyes on her white blouse, which had a yellow flower a few inches from the top. The blue skirt made her entire figure stand out.

Whenever they were out, she drank more than she should. She didn't have a favorite drink, she drank anything. There was a line of people outside the door waiting for a chance to enter the establishment.

He asked her what her future plans were to which she replied, "I am not sure right at the present. I am considering Europe."

She told him it was a place she always wanted to go. She sipped her Manhattan slowly and looked up at him, waiting for a response. He said nothing. She mentioned she would like to continue her education.

"You say you want to go to Europe to prolong your studies, but why Europe? There are excellent choices of colleges here in this country."

She was hinting to him that she would be away and wondered how he would receive it. She realized he wasn't moved by the thought of her traveling far away.

With a change of subject, he asked, "What is the difference between the south shore and the north shore?" She wasn't sure what he meant by his words. "I mean is it colder on the north shore or is it the same temperature?"

She explained, "Sometimes it's warmer on the north side and colder on the south." She smiled. "It all depends on the weather I assume."

They got up and danced for another twenty minutes before returning to their table. She ordered more drinks, which he wasn't in the mood for. She held her content of alcohol fairly well. Terrance was seeing a different personality than Erin's. This girl sitting across from him was completely opposite; they were two distinctly different people. Carolyn was unsure of herself; whereas, Erin had plans she followed to the letter. He knew that Carolyn had her good points. She was thoughtful and dependable. He loved this way of life and he could never see Erin having fun like this. Then he thought it might be her Catholic education that crippled her outlook on life. Carolyn took his hand at the table and asked him what he was thinking.

"You were miles away from me just now," she said.

He told her, "Please forgive me as I was daydreaming again. My mind returned to Ireland for a few seconds."

They finished their drinks and left. He told her it wasn't necessary for her to take him home; he would ride the train.

"I want you to come up to my apartment for just one more drink," she told him.

He said he had enough and wanted to go to bed and sleep for a week. Yet she drove to her apartment and said very little. When they arrived, she alighted from the auto and went over to his side of the door, reached in, and took his arm.

"Please," she begged, "just for a little while."

He was impressed with her home. There were four large rooms dressed with elegant furniture. He figured her parents had probably bought it for her.

"Let me get you a drink," she said.

He insisted he had enough for the night and told her he believed she had enough as well. He sat in one of those overstuff chairs that weighs a ton. She came over to him carrying her drink in a tall red glass. He had no idea what sort of alcohol was in it. She plopped herself into his lap and placed her arm around his neck. She asked him if he wanted her to put on the radio so they could hear the news flashes. She started to giggle and sing off tune. His mind was inflamed; she was the most luscious thing alive. She said nothing, but continued to smile at him. He took the glass out of her hand and placed it on the table next to him. He picked her up and carried her to the bedroom and, with his foot, kicked the door shut.

He awoke to feel her fingers playing with his hair at the bottom of his neck. They wore nothing. She had snuggled up next to him. She had placed her left leg over his leg while sleeping. Lying on his side, he could see outside the window and watched the large snowflakes flowing through the air. As she walked to the bathroom, she told him she was going to run a bath for them both.

17

Erin kept a keen eye on her new guest Carl Hosten to see how he would respond with the other guests. He was very talkative, and with his positive attitude, he mingled easily. Twice, he had dinner with the librarian at her table. Erin thought they would have a lot in common with their occupations. The couple said very little about their private life and talked mostly about the town and the lodge they now called home. How nice everyone seemed to get along and how they enjoyed each other's company. Once or twice they touched on her work at the library and what good books were available. Neither of them drank alcohol, preferring to stay with water or soft drinks. There were times they would go ten or fifteen minutes without speaking.

The evening newspapers were always on hand for the lodgers. The news was always bad, with no end in sight regarding the troubled economy. No work was available. Papers stated there was a man named Hitler in Germany calling for an uprising in his country. He demanded the land that was taken from Germany at the end of the First World War be returned.

Mr. Hosten implied there would never be any more wars in the world, telling Ms. Sinclare, "When the last war ended, it ended all wars. People are fed up with wars and all the killings and gassing." Sipping his hot tea he said, "The Germans deserved everything they received at the end of the war. They lost a good portion of their land and will never be able to rearm again. I guarantee you in a few months you won't hear Hitler's name again."

Though she never missed a word, the librarian said nothing.

When Erin came into the room, Ms. Sinclare thanked her for a delicious dinner. Erin sat and talked with the guests for a little while when the phone rang. It was Terrance and he explained he would be tied up with work the following weekend and wouldn't be able to make it over to the lodge as they had planned. She accepted his story but was rather concerned he would be missing this weekend as she had something special planned for him. Sunday was his birthday. He had missed visiting in the past, so she wondered if they were growing apart. Did they still have that special relationship? She knew there were times he wanted to touch her, be close to her. But did she ever once give him the implication she wanted him in that particular way? She knew she would miss him. She missed him even now. She wondered what he was doing in Boston by himself. Was he by himself? She had to remind herself that she had no holds on him. If he was seeing a girl, it was certainly his own business. All sorts of tumultuous thoughts ran through her mind. The more she thought of him not coming over this weekend, the more she became angry. What sort of work could he be doing on a Sunday? She left her guests and went into the kitchen to clean up.

Terrance's absence was still on her mind, but she decided not to dwell on it and put it out of her mind. She looked out the living room window and saw Mr. Hosten and Ms. Sinclare walking down the road toward town. Several guests were still in the dining room while others sat in the living room and listened to the radio. Radio was just coming alive and they were now broadcasting programs and not just music on the airwaves. Although news flashes were still in popular demand, radio was looking for fresh material to bring to the airwaves.

In the late nineteenth century, a wharf was built in the center of the village so boats could deliver their goods to the stores. The majority of the dry goods and food came from Boston or Revere. The wharf was eighty feet long and thirty feet wide, so it was a decent-size area for the people of Snugport to mingle with friends and shoot the breeze. It was a gathering place for those who love to gossip. With the wind blowing off the sea, it could be cold down by the wharf. Mr. Hosten and Ms. Sinclare sat at one of the benches and decided to rest after their brief walk from the lodge. The wharf was deserted at that time. Ms. Sinclare asked Hosten what his future plans were in town. He wasn't sure what the future held for him and he planned on taking it one day at a time. He never married and enjoyed life as it was. She too was never married.

"Do you regret it in any way? I mean . . . never having a husband or children. I hope you don't think I am being overly inquisitive," Mr. Hosten said.

"No, of course not," she replied, "but I am not sure how to answer you except to say that so far I have been happy doing what I love and that is working with books. I enjoy my friends and meeting new people. And I love to read. I believe I have handled not having a man in my life to my satisfaction. Then, of course, with a man I might have been happier. I cannot say for certain, for that is all speculation."

Hosten then told her she might have been *un*happy with a man. She said she wasn't sure she would be easy to live with now as she soon would be reaching middle age.

"I have been on my own too long. But if the right person came along, who knows what could occur."

Right now, however, she was freezing and she asked that they return to the manor. He placed his hand around her waist, guiding her along.

"We will have a nice cup of tea when we get back."

She said, "Good, and then you can tell me all about your teaching career and why you never married."

Terrance wrote to Peter in Downey Lock and was careful with what he revealed about what was happening in Boston. He said only that work was good and he was living in a nice apartment in Boston. He kept his writing low-key and didn't elaborate on anything personal.

The following day, Terrance called Erin and asked if she could meet him for lunch in Boston. She said she couldn't on that day but was free on Thursday if that was okay with him. They agreed to meet at his work site and ate at a little sandwich shop near the Boston Harbor. Over sandwiches and coffee, they both talked about what was happening between them. Erin hinted that it had been a while since she had last seen him. To Terrance, she looked the same, ever so lovely with that shining black hair. He took in her entire face, fascinated even by the way her eyebrows were perfect. She saw something in his face that puzzled her. It was different when he spoke. In the past, he always kept his eyes fixed on her, never avoiding eye contact. Now, when talking to her, he would look away for a moment or two then return his gaze. She wanted to know if everything was okay between them.

She explained, "It's just that I haven't seen you for a while. I've missed your company."

He replied, "I have been working longer hours, Erin. Since they let some workers go, it's been more difficult for me. Everyone has to do their part and pitch in with the work."

She knew it was a weak answer and so did he. He asked her about Albert Mandeville and how their courtship was getting along. She said it had ended but left it at that because she wasn't about to elaborate on what had transpired to cause the breakup. It was obvious he was very interested in the details, but now was not the time to discuss all the particulars surrounding the split. It would cause her too much embarrassment. He decided he would tell his friend about Carolyn and their affair.

She said, "When days went by and I didn't hear from you, I thought you might be seeing someone. But that's okay, why shouldn't you be seeing a girl of your choice." The way she took the news surprised him. There were no visibly hurt feelings and she maintained her mild disposition. Only once had he seen her angry and that was when they were children back in Downey Lock. It was when he scared her during their adventures in the caverns. But something told him she could be a real fireball if someone deliberately injured her pride. They made a date to meet again the following Saturday and visit some of the museums in Boston.

On the train home, she sensed there was more to the relationship between Terrance and Carolyn than Terrance let on. She resolved to leave the situation alone for now and see how it developed in the future. By now it was clear to her that she never had any deep feelings for Albert, and in hindsight, it might have been a mistake to mention him to Terrance when he first arrived in Snugport. She scolded herself for being so foolish. She should have opened herself up more to him, let him know she needed him. Now, it may be too late for them. She didn't want him to call on her because he felt responsible or because he felt obligated because of their past friendship.

One rainy afternoon, Carolyn came to see Terrance at the site where he was working. She looked tired and wasn't herself. He wanted to know if she was okay. He asked what was wrong.

She said, "I know you're busy, so I won't be long."

She had overheard her parents discussing how things weren't going well with the construction company. Money was tight and they were behind on some of the bills. She heard her father mention there were to be some more layoffs. On top of all that, she was feeling sick to her stomach and thought perhaps she had caught a touch of the flu.

"Go home. Get some rest," he suggested. "There is nothing we can do about anyone getting laid off. I have no control over a situation like that, Carolyn. Now please go home and rest the entire day. I will call you later."

The mention of layoffs, however, had worried him and he thought of asking Bernie Rufferson if there had indeed been word of another layoff, a layoff that might include him. He thought the better of it and left the matter alone for now. The fact that he would soon have to make a decision between the two ladies in his life still weighed heavily on his shoulders. Which of the two did he want to spend the rest of his life with? He enjoyed Carolyn's company and their lifestyle together. But was he in love with her? Was he in love with Erin? Both girls were a delight and genuinely grand people. Carolyn was very attached to her family and listened to everything they said. Erin was more independent and liked being on her own. Regarding his relative feelings toward the two, he was utterly confused.

That Saturday, he met Erin at the train station, and together, they took a taxi to Washington Street. Snow was falling lightly as they visited two of the Boston museums. For dinner, they visited a steak house down by the harbor. Afterward, they proceeded to a Speakeasy for drinks. She told him it was nice to have someone serve her for a change instead of having to cook and serve her own guests. Recently, she had hired a French girl to help with some of the cooking and baking. Her name was Emma Girard and she was twenty-seven with an enjoyable personality. Fortunately, Erin's place was booming and she was thinking about adding more rooms. Because of the economy, she wasn't sure if she could get a loan from the bank. Terrance enjoyed sitting across from this young beauty, taking in every word she uttered. The snow was coming down rather fast now and was covering the sidewalks. She still had on her blue woolen coat. He knew it was an inexpensive coat, not like anything Carolyn would dare be seen wearing. Completing her outfit was a green blouse with a short black skirt that fell just an inch below her knees. A piano player in front of them was humming out tunes. On every table lay a white tablecloth on which a lit candle was centered.

"Right now I can't think of a better place I would rather be than right here," he told her.

She smiled and said, "Do you say that to all the young ladies you bring out on the town?"

He touched her face with his hand. She took his hand and pressed it even closer to her cheek. He told her it had been a long time since Downey Lock.

She nodded and replied, "It's grand seeing you again."

She sipped her sparkling wine, and he could see that serious look she displayed whenever she had a significant issue she wanted to discuss.

"What is it, Erin?" he asked.

She replied, "Are you in love with Carolyn . . . I mean, is it really something you want?"

The last time they were together and talked, he didn't think it was that important to her. Now she was asking direct questions about his personal life. He told her she was the one that was having a relationship with Albert. He knew she wanted a truthful answer right now. She was in no mood to be put off. He had to speak from his heart and not his mind. He looked straight into her eyes and said, "Erin, I have loved you since we were kids way back in Downey Lock when I kicked the soccer ball into your face. I wasn't so sure you had the same feelings regarding me. I thought about you every minute of every day throughout the years. I wondered what it would be like to be together. But we were children then and now everything has changed. I still don't know your intentions and how you feel about me."

Her face didn't change; she still wore a serious expression. She spoke softly with words of tenderness and told him, "I have never forgotten you. You have always been with me. When you came to Boston and I saw you for the first time, my heart was full of love. I came back to reality and knew everything would be wonderful again between us. But I need to know, what are your intentions with Carolyn?"

Terrance replied, "She has been there for me ever since I have been in Boston. She is a nice person, but I realized from the beginning she and I would never be together forever. I will see her soon and explain everything about us. I am not sure how she will take it. I only hope she will understand how we feel. For now, let's get out of here." And they left.

Outside, there was an alley adjacent to the building and he took her arm and pulled her to him. He braced her against the wall and kissed her. The snow was covering their heads now. She responded to the kiss by holding him close to her. He asked her to come to his apartment for the night. She refused and whispered to him she had to get everything ready for the morning at the lodge. She asked him to take the train to her lodge and stay the night there. He thought for a moment and the idea of spending the evening with her appealed to him. She held the back of his head and ran her fingers through his hair. He wanted to go with her but wasn't sure it would be the right decision for him to make. When they kissed again, the decision was finalized. He took her arm and they proceeded to the train station. Even though the other three seats were vacant, he sat next to her on the train, so close that he didn't have to reach over to make contact with her. In this way, he was able to place his arm around her shoulder and cuddle her close to him. The snow had stopped, but looking out the window, he could see the howling wind was extremely strong. Terrance thought about what the night had to offer and couldn't help but smile at his Irish girl. She was wondering what was behind his smile but said nothing and held one of his hands.

The lodge was in darkness and everyone was sleeping. She took his hand and they went to her bedroom on the second landing. It was away from the guests at the end of a long hallway. She heard him mention something regarding Albert, but didn't get the full gist of what he said. Regardless, she quickly responded that Albert never touched her. "No one has ever laid a finger on me that way, Terrance."

He sat on the edge of the bed and looked up at her and held out his arms to her. He was smiling. She had no expression on her face. She came to him without any qualms, thinking she was giving herself for the first time to the man she loved.

When Terrance woke up and checked his wristwatch, it read 5:10 a.m. Erin was already up. He lay back, wanting more sleep. Why did she get up so early on a Sunday? He wanted her again. He heard footsteps in the hallway and then she opened the door.

She told him breakfast was waiting for him downstairs when he was ready. She had on a green apron. Even now, she was appealing to him. He sat on the edge of the bed still naked from the night before. Even though she didn't say anything, he could tell she was embarrassed. He asked her to sit next to him on the bed. Seeing that he wanted her again, she closed the door and walked toward him.

Terrance found a letter in his mailbox written by Father McVey from Ireland. It contained the following:

Dear Terrance:

I was able to get your address from Peter and thought it best I write you. I hope this letter finds you in the best of health and you are doing well in your new employment. I understand Erin is happy and is enjoying New England. I am afraid I have some rather bad news for you. Terrance, your friend and guidance teacher Brother John has passed on. Over a year ago, he returned to Northern Ireland, to a small village twenty miles from Belfast. The people connected with the IRA brought him back to assist them in another of their missions. I was told by other religious members he didn't want to go back, but felt obligated to help them out this one last time. There were four individuals involved in the plot. They were to rob a bank and get to a safe house a few miles away. Brother John was to do the driving as he is noted to be the best getaway driver in all of Ireland. I was informed that in the past he had been the driver on several other bank robberies. I was told the police were waiting for them at the bank when the three of them approached the front entrance. Someone tipped them off. No one knows who shot first, but the three at the front entrance were killed immediately. When Brother John attempted to drive off, they sprayed his car with bullets and he crashed into a pole. He later died at the hospital.

I know this is horrible news for you to receive. Somehow, you would have found out and I wanted to tell you first. He was buried in a cemetery outside of Belfast. I feel sorry for your sadness right now. If there is anything I can do to help in this situation, please do not hesitate to write me.

Yours Truly

Father McVey.

Terrance sat down on the stoop still holding the letter. As he thought of Ireland and his mentor, tears glistened in his eyes. He always knew there was something mysterious about Brother John. It was like he constantly wanted to conceal his past. He never mentioned anything regarding Northern Ireland or being affiliated with any such organization. He never gave the impression he had a hidden agenda or was deeply involved in politics. At that moment, there were a thousand things running through Terrance's mind. It didn't really matter how his friend ended up, he still thought the world of his Catholic mentor. Terrance knew the brother would never entirely leave his life and he would always remember him as his trusted friend. Terrance believed that if it weren't for Brother John, there is no telling where he might have ended up. While sobbing and, with both hands buried in his face, he thought of his grand friend once again.

The next day Terrance called Carolyn and she picked him up at work and drove to his apartment. He knew this wasn't going to be an easy task. He told her everything about himself and Erin. The entire time he talked, she never interrupted him. Finally, she got up from the kitchen chair and walked over to one of the large windows in the room. Gazing out the window, she said she had some news for him too.

She said, "I'm pregnant with your baby. I went to a specialist, not my family doctor, because I didn't want my parents to know. He confirmed it. Anyway, I knew when I was late this month. What do you propose we should do about my condition?"

It was as if he had been hit by a large truck. His life was about to drastically change. A woman he did not love would be in his life forever. The child would need a father to take care of him. He knew he was the father. No one else was in the picture. She asked why he wasn't saying anything, if he had any questions.

"Are you thinking perhaps you are not the father?" she asked.

Terrance replied, "Of course not."

She told him she was sorry that this put him in a difficult situation. She walked over to him and placed her hands around his neck and told him she loved him no matter what.

"I know you are not in love with me, but I don't care. I do know I really need and want you here by my side right now. Of course, I can't make you. It will have to be your decision."

She thought for a moment and then told him she was going home to tell her parents everything. He watched from his window as she got into her automobile and drove rapidly from his sight.

Spring would be coming soon. A robin had already been spotted in the area. March on the north shore can be just as cold as the middle of January. Terrance informed Erin he had things he had to talk over with her and he was taking the train to Snugport tomorrow after work. He arrived just before seven in the evening. The guests at the lodge were still having dinner. Erin was happy to see him again so soon. He went to the liquor cabinet in the kitchen and poured some whiskey into a glass. He waited until Erin could take a break from her chores. She was anxious to see what news he brought with him. He finally told her everything that transpired between Carolyn and him. She looked at him and said,

"And you believe her?"

"Why shouldn't I believe her? She isn't lying."

"Terrance, you have no idea if she is telling you the truth or if she wants you for herself. She will do anything to keep you. I don't believe her."

Terrance replied, "You don't even know her." At that point, she asked him point-blank what his intentions were.

"I am going to do the honorable thing and marry her. I'm sorry, Erin. You have no idea how so very sorry I am for us."

She said nothing and then went to the dining room and brought back some dinner dishes. He spoke again and told her that he had thought the entire situation over and it was the only honorable thing to do. The baby will need a name and a father.

She turned and informed him, "The last train leaves for Boston in twelve minutes. You better leave now or you will miss it."

On the train back to Boston, he pondered whether he made the correct choice. He wondered if this would end any kind of relationship with Erin. It certainly didn't appear prosperous. He knew it had to be done, and at a time like this, the baby came first. He just wanted to get to his apartment and sleep. Everything was happening too fast.

Carolyn's mother called and asked him to come over the following evening. He knew to expect the worst. All three sat in the living room. There wasn't anything further to explain. Everyone there knew why there was a meeting. Terrance didn't hesitate and informed Carolyn's parents he would marry their daughter. He hoped it didn't sound like he was doing them a favor. How do you say something like that and have it come out the right way? Both parents expressed their feelings, saying both Terrance and Carolyn were responsible for what occurred. Terrance believed Carolyn's father was hurting more than her mother. Mrs. Rosetelli told him she and her husband had plans for Carolyn and it appeared now these plans would have to be put on hold.

"She has ruined herself," stammered Mr. Rosetelli. "This news will spread all over Boston. Who knows how far! It is a total mess and an extreme embarrassment to our entire family."

Mr. Rosetelli glared at Carolyn and told her there would be no further schooling or fun in Europe. Soon, she would have a child to care for. Terrance could see that he had been drinking, as every now and then, he would mispronounce a word. His face was flushed with anger as he spoke. Carolyn said she and Terrance would get to work planning the marriage. She hoped it would occur within the next month.

The room was so quiet it was like a funeral parlor the morning the deceased was to be buried. Carolyn told Terrance she would drive him home.

Her father said, "Let him walk."

They said nothing until she drove up to his apartment.

She said, "I know this is a horrible situation for you. It's not an easy one for me either."

He asked her if she was in love with him.

She replied, "I am not sure. Before all this happened, I thought I was. I just don't know anymore."

He opened the door to leave when she took his arm and said, "Don't run out on me. I need you. Forget about returning to Ireland."

A couple of weeks went by without Terrance hearing a word from Carolyn or her family.

He called Erin's lodge asking for her, but her assistant excused her each time, saying she was out or couldn't come to the phone. He kept working every day and everything seemed normal during working hours. Workers were laying a concrete foundation on one of the buildings adjacent to the site where he had been working. Terrance was instructing the workers how to complete the job when Bernie Rufferson approached him. Rufferson informed him that Carolyn Rosetelli had been in the hospital for the last two days. She had a miscarriage and was at Boston's Mercy Hospital. Immediately, he left for the hospital. Both Louis and Claire Rosetelli were in the room. Carolyn was sitting in a chair. She reached up for him and started to cry. Mr. and Mrs. Rosetelli walked out of the room without speaking.

Terrance said, "I didn't know. I am so sorry. I just found out today."

She continued to cry while Terrance knelt down and held her hand. She buried her face into his chest and he patted her head. She told him it would have been a girl. He tried his best to comfort her, saying things such as these happen and there is nothing anyone can do about it. The following day, Terrance was fired from his job.

Carolyn called him later that week. They went to lunch down by the harbor. It was spring and the sun was brighter in the sky and everything was growing green. They sat by a large window so they could take in the view of the water and the brightness of the sun. It had been a lousy, cold, and snowy winter. Carolyn wanted him to know she was leaving for Europe in a few days. He told her he didn't have any specific plans right now and was attempting to get a job somewhere in, or at least close to, Boston. If he didn't find work soon, he might have to return to Ireland where he knew he could find some. There was no work and people were selling apples and in bread lines. She asked about Erin and he replied it was over between them. There wasn't anything more to say. She got up and gave him a kiss on the cheek, smiled, and left.

He looked for employment but was unsuccessful. Louis Rosetelli had put out word not to hire him under any circumstances. He had a lot of influence over other construction companies. The Rosetelli name was powerful in the state of Massachusetts.

Erin was approached by one of the leading bakeries in the Boston area and was asked if she had any interest in franchising her baked goods, to which she had added homemade meat and pork pies. Her fruit pies were still in heavy demand in the area and were now being requested in several other cities outside of Boston. While she wouldn't be responsible for the baking of the goods, but only for supplying the recipes, her name would be placed on all goods sold. She contacted her lawyer in Boston and was told by him that the income would be significant and would leave her secure and comfortable. The larger pies would probably cost a quarter and the smaller ones a nickel. She agreed and the signing was to occur the following day.

Carl Hosten and Dorothy Sinclare were walking on the beach after having a fulfilling dinner. They had grown close and were seldom apart. He spent many hours at the village library. They were well-known in town being seen often on the village green. It was on the village green, on a spring night, when he told her what happened at the school. "I was in charge of finances on the school board for five years when $3,000 went missing. The money was stolen from a safe to which I had the combination. I was directly accused of stealing the money by several teachers. You have to understand I was not the most popular teacher at the school. I had a few minor brushes with other teachers. I haven't got the sweetest disposition and some think I have a superior attitude. They asked me to resign, and in turn, they would not involve the police. I insisted on a police investigation, and one was held. I left during the investigation because the students at the school were making a laughing joke of me. The police found the real culprit. It was a young teacher who had only been at the school for three months. Somehow, he was able to open the safe. Of course, I was asked to return, complete with all their apologies and sympathy. They even asked me to stay on the school board, but I couldn't go back there. I was hated by most of them. They were all scared I was going to sue them."

As he reached the end of his story, Dorothy had tears in her eyes. She took his hand and told him he should have gone back if only to annoy them with his presence. He told her it was so nice and refreshing to finally have someone who believed in him. He wanted her to know that he not only respected her, but felt truly alive in her company.

Erin received the news of Carolyn's miscarriage the day after from her foster mother. Stella told her what she heard and wanted to know what she was going to do now.

"I am not going to do anything. Why should I?" said Erin.

Stella continued, "Several days ago, I was told Terrance was fired from his job and he is unable to find work. He is thinking about returning to Ireland."

Stella knew Erin was confused and could also be very stubborn. Stella told her not to hide her true feelings that only she herself would know how she felt regarding this situation.

Erin thanked her for her advice and said, "When I was living with you, you always let me make my own decisions. I will do what is best for me now."

Terrance's money was running out and he had to make a decision soon. He thought it would be best to return to Downey Lock, he hated to go back as a failure. Terrance took the afternoon train to Snugport. He was determined to see her one last time. There would be no explaining or apologizing for anything. He told himself he would keep his feelings out of their conversation. He thought now that Erin hated him. The walk from the village to the seaside lodge took only minutes. He saw Stella and stopped and waved to her.

She waved and shouted, "It is wonderful to see you again, Terrance."

The June heat was early this year, but nevertheless welcomed. He saw Erin on the beach looking out at the sea. He climbed down the stairs to the beach when she turned and saw him and greeted him with a smile. She ran toward him and he met her halfway and she jumped into his arms. They hugged and then kissed. She buried her face into his neck.

Then she asked, "What the bloody hell kept you?"

Holding hands, they walked out toward the surf. He explained that just yesterday he was thinking about going back to Ireland.

"You're not going anywhere," she told him. "Anyway, my bicycle is broken again." They both laughed. He put his arm around her waist.

"We are going to need a new roof on the lodge soon," said Erin.

Three months later, they were married. A large reception was held at their home on the ocean. Only nine months later, Erin had a child, a boy they named Jack.

（

Made in United States
North Haven, CT
10 June 2024

53419196R10114